P9-DTL-569

BELLE HAVEN

BELLE

HAVEN

Juliet Fitzgerald

VIKING

VIKING

Published by the Penguin Group
Viking Penguin, a division of Penguin Books USA Inc.,
375 Hudson Street, New York, New York 10014, U.S.A.
Penguin Books Ltd, 27 Wrights Lane, London W8 5TZ, England
Penguin Books Australia Ltd, Ringwood, Victoria, Australia
Penguin Books Canada Ltd, 2801 John Street,
Markham, Ontario, Canada L3R 1B4
Penguin Books (N.Z.) Ltd, 182–190 Wairau Road,
Auckland 10, New Zealand

Penguin Books Ltd, Registered Offices:
Harmondsworth, Middlesex, England

First published in 1990 by Viking Penguin,
a division of Penguin Books USA Inc.

1 3 5 7 9 10 8 6 4 2

LIBRARY OF CONGRESS CATALOGING IN PUBLICATION DATA
Fitzgerald, Juliet.
Belle Haven / Juliet Fitzgerald.
p.   cm.
ISBN 0–670–83318–5
I. Title.
PS3556.I8325B45   1990
813'.54—dc20   90–50044

Printed in the United States of America
Set in Garamond No. 3

This book is for
Meg Ruley
tanti auguri, amica mia

And all that Memory loves the most
   Was once our only Hope to be,
And all that Hope adored and lost
   Hath melted into Memory.

Alas! it is delusion all;
   The future cheats us from afar
Nor can we be what we recall,
   Nor dare we think on what we are.

                    —Byron

Part I

1

Belle Haven they called it. Belle hell, I say. I'm near blind now and my fingers tremble as I hold this pen, but seventy years, seventy lifetimes will not banish Belle Haven from my vision as I saw it that May afternoon, enthroned in the Virginia hills. The architecture of immense satisfaction best describes Belle Haven, a study in the symmetry of wealth. Bay windows billowed like crinoline on either side of the massive mahogany doors. White and high as a three-tiered wedding cake, Belle Haven's windows gleamed in the western sun, the handsome facade unmarred by anything so cozy as a porch. Shaded verandas were tucked in the back so that the house could regard the world with unencumbered aplomb. Tired, dusty, disgraced, I stood on the road that May day in 1921 and looked up at Belle Haven. Even from that distance I could tell Belle Haven disapproved of me. I girded myself for the ordeal I knew lay ahead. But in truth, I knew nothing of what lay ahead.

I could have called from the train station in Oakstone and the chauffeur would have picked me up, but the bus seemed more in keeping with my ignominious return. Besides, I had no reason to believe that this sojourn at Belle Haven would be different from any of my other brief stays; clearly, I would but stop at Belle Haven while my Aunt Charlotte decided what was to be done with me. By now she had no doubt received the letter from the dean expelling me from Merrywell College for Women. I'd always thought the college appropriately named because, above all, the students were expected to marry well, preferably boys from one of the numerous men's schools nearby.

The huge gates at the foot of the mile-long drive were closed and locked with a BH entwined in a heart of wrought iron. All the locks at Belle Haven were heart-shaped. So, I slid down the ravine carrying my suitcase, my music satchel, and my flute—all I possessed in the world, splashed through the muddy creek at the bottom of the hill, and clambered back up. I tried to scrape the mud from my shoes and to rub the grass stain from my stockings, but there was nothing to be done about them, and I made my way up the long drive. The last of the white dogwood blossoms fell over me like gentle confetti.

The gardens surrounding the house were ablaze with azaleas, and battalions of flowers protected the bay windows. The house was quiet, but never empty, not with the many servants required to keep it running smoothly. As I faced the huge mahogany doors, I debated going round to the servants' entrance, but felt I should show some courage now or else I would cower forever. Still, I couldn't bring myself simply to walk in. I put down my suitcase and rang the bell.

The door was opened by the most beautiful man I've ever seen, before or since. He wore the stiff formal black of a butler's garb, but the sobriety of his clothes only served to set off his porcelain complexion, flawless save for a brush of rose where his high cheek bones met his sculpted temples. A thatch of smooth blond hair lay across his head. His lips were full, and his eyes enormous, blue and icy as shallow water in winter.

"I'm Dabney Beale," I announced.

"Miss?"

"Mrs. Courtney's niece, Dabney Beale."

His eyes looked even more vacant, but he opened the door and told me to wait in the hall while he went to announce me to Charlotte. All of my aunts insisted I call them by their first names. They believed that "Aunt" had a chummy, nursery-like ring, which Charlotte in particular found intolerable. It was not difficult to comply with their request, since none of my aunts was the least bit chummy and all of them would have been out of place in a nursery.

I set my suitcase on the parquet floor and my flute and music satchel on the table, beside a large Chinese vase full of white roses. White roses were Charlotte's favorite; she grew them in shades of ivory, oyster, pearl—and these, a delicate snowflake white. I ran my fingers over their petals and searched in vain for a scent.

The beautiful young man returned to the hall. "Mrs. Courtney is on the patio with Mr. Duckworth and she'll see you."

"Thank you, Mr. . . ."

"Favour. James Favour."

I followed him through the glassed doors, which opened into the rose garden. To the left was the sun room, a small but bountiful greenhouse where Charlotte sat in winter, and to the right, the flagstone patio, set about with potted palms and draped with feathery ferns.

My aunt Charlotte lay draped on a chaise, dressed in a crepe de chine tennis dress with a madonna blue scarf around her hair. Her long legs were crossed casually, but Charlotte could never look relaxed; there was too much static electricity about her. Even her clothes crackled as she moved to greet me and gave me her hand that smelled—as she had always smelled—of Rappaccini cologne, expensive, bottled in bond, volatile, 190 proof.

"Dabney my dear, what a surprise. Why didn't you ring us

or wire us you were coming? That will be all, Favour," she said to the butler, who was frozen like a marble statue before us. "Tell Ethel there will be one more for dinner and have Marian fix up the east bedroom for Dabney." She moved back the chaise and wrapped her fingers around a sweating martini. She plucked the olive from the glass and put it between her glowing red lips and tossed the toothpick to the floor. "Sit down and relax, Dabney. You look awful, as usual. Navy blue and off-white," she scoffed, "suited only for the playing fields." She reached to the table beside her and dipped her hand into a silver bowl filled with chunks of raw meat. Carelessly, she tossed a piece of meat to Caesar, her bloodhound, an odious, spoiled, and surly beast if ever there was one. "Would you like a drink, Dabney? It's the last decent gin in America, isn't it, Eugene?"

"Hello, Dabney," said Eugene.

"You remember Eugene, of course."

"Of course." How could I forget Eugene Duckworth? He was as much a fixture at Belle Haven as the plumbing—and as essential. He was Charlotte's lawyer and business adviser, and he looked the type: gaunt, graying, with a long mouth and square jaw. He had been at Belle Haven as long as I could remember; he even had his own room. He always treated me with a reserve that bordered on disdain, and I returned his contempt. I thought him horribly hairy, with his hairy hands, and little tufts of hair in his ears and nose.

"Speak of the devil, isn't that what they say?" said Charlotte, refilling her glass from the martini pitcher. "Eugene and I were just discussing you, Dabney. Don't blush. God! Don't blush. It makes you look so infernally young. Did you fail blushing at Merrywell College? Is that why they expelled you one week before the end of the term?"

"Didn't the dean tell you why I was expelled?"

"The dean said something about your having broken Merrywell's Code of Honor and having committed acts despicable beyond description. Eugene and I were just wondering what could be that wonderfully despicable. Eugene thought you might have been fornicating on the Founder's Tomb. Was that it?"

Charlotte laughed in a good-natured way, and even Eugene's stony countenance twitched with mirth. I could not help blushing all the more, since, as they well knew, fornicating was not a word I was accustomed to hearing. I had a pretty good idea of what transpired between men and women and it had ceased to repel me, but at nineteen my virginity was still intact and, indeed, had never been seriously endangered, because all the young men who courted Merrywell girls were gentlemen—which simply meant that their assaults on us were drunken, short-lived, brutish, and that they always apologized afterward.

Eugene helped himself to another martini. His eyes flickered over me swiftly, and involuntarily I looked away. Eugene never missed a thing.

"Really, Dabney, what did you do?" Charlotte continued. "It must have been pretty awful for Merrywell to expel you and risk losing the Fairchild endowment. Even Merrywell can't afford to spurn money. Maybe I'll call the dean and threaten to withdraw the Fairchild endowment and she'll let you back in."

"I don't want to go back. I hate Merrywell College and I wouldn't go back if they begged me!"

"Oh my! Did you hear that, Eugene? The little beggar thinks she's a chooser. And where else did you think you might go, miss? Your grades aren't exactly enough to ingratiate you with Vassar." She tossed another piece of meat to the slavering Caesar.

"I don't want to go to Vassar."

"My dear, I should warn you, it is immaterial to me what you want. I am your guardian and you'll do as I tell you."

"Only till I'm twenty-one! I'm free when I'm twenty-one."

"Free," she cooed. "Listen to that, Eugene. You'll be free of me when I say so, Miss Dabney Beale, and don't you forget it. Now"—she took a long sip of martini. Charlotte always seemed surprised when emotion—any emotion—crept up on her. She continued more calmly. "Tell me why you were expelled from Merrywell College. What was so deliciously despicable?"

"I refused to rat on my friend," I announced.

"I wish you wouldn't speak in the inexplicable vernacular. What exactly do you mean—rat on your friend?"

"They thought I had an accomplice and I said I did not and they didn't believe me, so they expelled me."

"An accomplice in what?"

I twisted my fingers in my lap. Though I had been rehearsing this speech from the moment I left Merrywell, it still would not be easy. "It had to do with a cow," I began.

"A cow!" snorted the usually taciturn Eugene.

"There is a dairy near Merrywell and one night we—I—borrowed a cow from the dairy and let it into the library. It was all done in fun."

"And what did you do with this cow in the library? Introduce it to Jane Austen?"

"We—I—took it to the second floor."

"To improve its mind?"

"No, just for fun."

"Is pushing a cow's rump up the stairs very amusing, then?" Charlotte regarded me archly.

"We didn't have to push it up. It went up by itself. It's just that—"

"That?"

"It wouldn't come down by itself. Cows won't go down stairs."

"And when did you add that little morsel of knowledge to your experience?"

"The next day," I said miserably. "The dairyman was there,

the newspaper, the police, everyone, but they couldn't persuade the cow to go down, so they had to get a winch and lower it."

Eugene laughed so hard he choked on his olive and Charlotte had to pound him on the back. Even Caesar regarded me with renewed interest. "How were you caught in this desperate act?"

By my sniveling rat of a roommate, I wanted to say, but didn't. I simply said that the library keys were found in my possession. Of course, if I'd had a grain of sense, I would have thrown the keys in the bushes, but I hadn't that much presence of mind as we left the library, laughing and enjoying the vision of what would happen the next day. Three days after the cow had been removed from the library my roommate searched my desk, found the keys, and took them to the dean. I was indicted and convicted of having stolen the keys and introducing the cow into the library, but I was expelled for not informing on my accomplice. (Who shall still remain nameless. She married into a famous Virginia family and I doubt they'd find it funny. Even now.)

"Weren't you the noble one," said Charlotte, finishing off the last of the martinis. "I suppose next you'll tell me it was a far, far better thing than you have ever done before."

"I didn't think they'd expel me," I confessed.

"Because of all the money the Fairchilds have given to Merrywell, is that it?"

"Yes," I admitted.

"Ah, Eugene, is that not one of life's hardest lessons? To know the limits of one's power. Even money can't protect you from everything, can it, Eugene?"

"So they say."

Charlotte studied me and I began to blush anew. "However, you'd think that money could at least ensure a little good taste. You have the most awful clothes, Dabney. You look worse than Marian." Marian was the maid at Belle Haven; she was always slovenly, her hem falling out, her stockings drooping, but she was tolerated because she was literally mute. In that sense she was as indispensable as a eunuch in a harem, and she had been at Belle Haven as long as I could remember.

"Well, Eugene, you write a response to the dean and I'll sign it. You might want to hint that we will withdraw the Fairchild endowment. There are other things I could be doing with that money." She rose and stretched. "I want to take a bath before dinner. We'll discuss this cow business later."

"I'm sorry," I said reflexively.

"Yes, well, sorry never buttered anyone's bread." She gave me a hard look and rose; Eugene and Caesar followed her into the house.

My aunt and Eugene were probably about the same age, but Eugene looked all of forty-five and Charlotte did not, partially because she was skilled with a makeup brush. She had been slender and willowy as a girl, but had become flint thin as a woman, as if age had taken a scalpel to her and sliced away the fullness from her body and face, sharpened her edges, accentuating her cheekbones, her chin, and her arrogance. She wore her hair bobbed daringly in a helmet of gold with one curl free, which fell seductively over her left eye. Her eyes—the famous Fairchild eyes—were dark brown with glints of gold. All the Fairchild beauties, the four sisters—Charlotte, Julia, Francesca, and Alicia—had those famous eyes. One of their many suitors was a poet whose tribute to their eyes may still be found in anthologies of the day.

As a young girl I had spent many futile hours in front of the mirror looking for a glimpse of the Fairchild gold in my own eyes, but by the time I was nineteen I had given up and reconciled myself to being plain and ungainly. Like the other Fairchild beauties, I had a long neck and long legs and a high forehead, but my hair was pale, sandy and nondescript, and my green eyes must have come from my father. These eyes have served me for nearly ninety years and I have long since ceased to begrudge them their lack of Fairchild gold. Besides, I know now that the Fairchild gold was only a reflection of what the Fairchild money could—and did—buy.

I needed no guide to my room. I always had the same one when I stayed at Belle Haven, and I sighed with relief as I started up the staircase and smiled to remember how the teakwood balustrade had always reminded me of a treble clef sign. At least Charlotte was not furious; moreover, I was free of Merrywell College. She would not make me go back. The first breath of evening blew into the hall and up the stairs and brought with it relief, a sense of pleasant harmony at that moment. I was, after all, young and resilient.

"Murderer! Murder!" cried a voice I knew all too well. Glass smashed and shattered on the landing. I heard Charlotte's footsteps fly overhead and saw the flash of her mauve dressing gown. "He's trying to poison me. Help! Murderer! You'll not kill me, you murdering lout. God will avenge his servants! The wicked shall perish!"

"Stop it, Austin," Charlotte commanded. "Stop it this minute."

"You've sent him to kill me. You!" he screamed. "I shall not be destroyed. Yea, it is the wicked and unrighteous who shall go down to destruction." His voice lost its quaver and uncertainty. "Go ye upon the walls and destroy—destroy!"

"Shut up, you blubbering fool," snapped Charlotte and her hand audibly cracked across Austin's cheek. Gasps and sobs sounded from him. "You may go now, Favour," said Charlotte in the same authoritative tone. "Mr. Courtney won't be needing anything else. Tell Ethel he will take his dinner in his room. Do you hear me? Favour!"

"But the glass?" Favour whispered plaintively.

"Clean it up later. Just get out. Do as I tell you."

"Yes, Mrs. Courtney."

The door closed behind her, muffling Austin's sobs, but the pitch and quality of Charlotte's invective rang even through the walls and echoed on the stairwell. As he descended, Favour met me on the stairs, but his reflectionless blue eyes did not return my furtive greeting.

I was born in England, the daughter of Julia Fairchild and the artist Anthony Dabney Beale, in the last year of Queen Victoria's reign, 1901. My birth and her death were almost simultaneous; the world I entered was draped in funereal pall. Since I was virtually given my father's name, Dabney Antonia Beale, I have no doubt that they wanted a son, but I was the only child of that ill-fated couple.

I have almost no recollection of my father, a good artist who longed to be a great one. In order to make ends meet, he painted many society women, but even those commissions fell off when, as my mother told me later, he refused to make the women lovely. "I'm only an artist," he told one husband, irate at the portrayal of his wife's weak chin, "not God. Talk to God if you want a beautiful wife." But my father's serious work was much regarded by his peers. In fact, my mother told me that my first visitor was the great James Whistler, who painted a small impromptu portrait of me. My first and only.

I never saw the Whistler portrait; it was sold that same year for a fraction of what it would have later brought. My mother said we needed the money for bread on the table and tea in the pot and that no one—not even my father—could eat paint, drink turpentine, or shelter a family with art. Yet they were happy in those early London days, but after my father's death in 1904 (he was run down by a hansom cab one especially foggy night), my mother scraped together enough money for a third-class passage to New York, where we took an apartment and she gave music lessons—piano and flute—for a living. Such as it was. I was happy enough, but she wasn't. I remember her strained face and forced smile, and the chill in our apartment that rendered her fingers useless for the piano or the flute—the chill, no doubt in her heart, that made music seem a mockery. She had brought many of my father's paintings with us to New York and tried to sell them there, but the work of an unknown British painter was worth even less in America than it was in Britain. A few passed to interested collectors, but the rest stayed rolled in a corner of our bedroom. I have no idea what happened to them after she died.

She died of pneumonia in a public ward of a charity hospital. I was eight. "Whatever they tell you," she said, clutching my hand, "never forget that you are the daughter of a great artist. Maybe not a great man, but who can say?"

"Who can say what, Mama? Who? What?"

She turned her gray face to me and spoke with a sudden ferocity that was underscored by her fever-bright eyes. "Whatever else you do in life, Dabney, don't let your own pride keep you from what you want. Do you hear me?" She seemed to shout as if I were far away, though in fact she was the one far away and those were the last lucid words she spoke.

Two days later our apartment was invaded by three tall, beautiful women all dressed in black. They introduced themselves to the stunned neighbors as Julia's sisters and my aunts. I took refuge in my favorite place, behind the skirt that hid the inadequate kitchen plumbing from view. It was damp and drippy down there, but the calico skirt was so thin that if I squinted, I could see through it, watching my aunts weep by the piano as they inspected the cold, grimy flat. They muttered about "poor dear Julia." And all agreed it "was all his fault." They spoke in hushed silken, rustling tones like their clothes. I wrapped my arms around my knees and huddled beneath the sink wondering what "it" was.

When they finally found me, they dusted me off and said what a fright I'd given them. They peered uneasily under the sink to see what might be coming out of the woodwork. Then they told me I was coming to Belle Haven to live. I had never heard of Belle Haven, though they found this incredible. Suffering loss, fatigue, bewilderment, I allowed myself to be removed from the apartment. I longed only for the refuge under the kitchen sink, but I never again found such a satisfactory hiding place.

After the comforting confines of the small apartment I shared with my mother, the expanse and population of Belle Haven were frightening. Besides the many servants and an almost endless stream of local gentry and out-of-town guests, there was Aunt Francesca, Aunt Alicia, Aunt Charlotte and her husband (a man who, so far as I know, had no other name than Doctor). My grandmother lived there too, though she didn't really count. She was reclusive in the extreme and when she died the following year, no one missed her. My grandfather was quite a different case. Who could mistake or ignore Charles Wilbur Fairchild? Master of Belle Haven. Patron of the Arts. Leader of the Hunt. Gentleman.

No one dared mention that the foundation of the family fortune lay in a lowly product, Grippit Glue. Ruthlessly advertised with the most extravagant claims, Grippit Glue opened the door to all of Grandfather's other enterprises, products, and undertakings. He came from some undistinguished place, arriving in Virginia (like so many others) after the Civil War armed only with ambition. Shrewdly Charles

Fairchild sensed the power of advertising long before it was known to all and he reckoned (correctly, clearly) on human vanity. He seemed to know that however poor and puny people's lives were, they always longed for grace and beauty. He made his fortune off that volatile combination of vanity and imagination because he offered people (particularly the poor and puny) the possibility of achieving grace and beauty, if only they would use his Rosebud Soap, Snow White Tooth Powder, Vita Bath Hair Restorer, the Electrolyzer Chin Strap, and many other such products. He hired a number of able managers so that he could distance himself from the plebeian source of his money. To mask the dull foundations of his empire, Grandfather became a great patron of the arts. Lavish concerts were held in the Belle Haven salon, and art work studded the walls and gardens. He built two guest cottages at the edge of the boxwood gardens—one to house a worthy poet for a year and one to house a worthy painter. Grandfather himself interviewed the candidates for his largesse, but when the painter Anthony Beale ran off with my mother, Julia Fairchild, the practice was discontinued and the cottages razed.

My grandfather took enormous pleasure in his four beautiful daughters; he had given them all lovely romantic names and they lived up to his expectations. From the time they were children they sat frequently for group and individual portraits, which were hung all over the house. The best of these were the four individual portraits painted by Anthony Beale, and however much Grandfather might have hated him for running off with Julia, all four portraits remained hanging in the salon, the grandest room in the house.

When my aunts brought me to Belle Haven they ushered me into the salon to meet my grandfather. He stood beside one of the marble-lipped fireplaces, still dressed in his riding clothes, his boots spattered with mud. I remember the boots particularly because I was afraid to look at his face. His sole comment was: "She's no beauty. She doesn't look like any of us."

Apparently he included himself in that legacy of beauty, though to my childish mind he was far from lovely: tall, bony-handed, with a thickly fleshed face and skin the yellowish color of aging paper.

When he died suddenly in 1911 they dressed me in black and told me I must be strong and not cry. Small chance of that. To me he was remote, austere, and unfeeling. He once flung his fork at me across the dinner table because I put my own knife into the butter, ignoring the butter knife placed there for that purpose. His fork missed me by inches. They did not have to tell me not to do that again.

I was neither lovely nor, as the saying goes, blithe and bonny, good and gay. In fact, amongst themselves my aunts referred to me as "Wednesday's Child"—full of woe—and they packed me off to boarding school. I went to several boarding schools, all called Miss So and So's Academy or variations on that theme. I returned to Belle Haven for holidays, some vacations, for the funerals of my grandparents, and for the weddings of my aunts, each a lavish society affair, or at least their first marriages were.

After they married, Alicia and Francesca left Belle Haven (though they always returned in between marriages). I spent some vacations in France with Alicia when she was married to an exiled (and as it turned out, penniless) Russian count and some vacations in California with Francesca when she was married to a film producer who affected a monocle and a European accent. I had some cousins born of these unions, though they were so much younger than I that we could not be friends. Even when they were very small and I reached out to touch their downy heads, a nanny inevitably came along and chastised me for "mussing them up."

Charlotte, the only childless Fairchild, stayed on at Belle Haven and was appointed my legal guardian. In the summer of 1914 I returned to Virginia for my summer vacation and found that two seemingly minor events had transpired—each of which would profoundly affect my life. Charlotte's husband, the kindly but aloof Doctor, had died in the spring (though no one had so much as mentioned this in a letter); secondly, Charlotte had built a bona fide swimming pool (complete with marble statuary) just beyond the east veranda. The pool itself meant nothing to me, but after it was built, no one ever swam at the Belle Haven lake again. The lake, forever deserted, passed to me, as it were, and I was left in sole possession of my very own kingdom.

The lake was at the very edge of Belle Haven's property, surrounded and protected by thickly wooded hills. Some seven miles away was the town of Oakstone, but no one from the town or the house ever disturbed the serenity of the lake. It was there I spent the happiest, the only unblighted, moments of my youth. It lay far beyond the boxwood gardens and tennis courts, in the opposite direction from the stables and the servants' quarters. The lake was quite large, maybe a mile wide, with two docks and three lovely little rowboats, the *Charlotte,* the *Alicia,* and the *Francesca.* (The *Julia,* I later learned, was ordered sunk, and it lay in the muck at the bottom of the lake.) There was a combined boathouse and bathhouse and a long diving board. Even in the dead of winter I would walk to the lake, where the little boats would be held motionless in the wafer-thin ice. And in the summer I swam for hours, danced out to the edge of the diving board, or best of all, rowed out to the center of the lake and lay in the bottom of the boat. Sometimes I read or played the flute, but more often I lay with my hands beneath my head and watched the porous clouds roll overhead as I was rocked to sleep by the lake's gentle hand.

When I returned to Belle Haven for the Christmas holidays in 1914, Charlotte herself met me at the Oakstone station, accompanied by a large, ruddy, good-looking man in a fur coat—the first I'd ever seen on a man. She introduced him to me as my Uncle Austin and said she had married him the month before.

Austin Courtney delighted me from the beginning. He was the first, indeed the only, occupant of Belle Haven (except for the distant and now dead Doctor) who didn't think my plainness a crime against the Fairchilds. He was kind, forthcoming, but best of all he talked back to Charlotte and whenever she began one of her tirades, he'd shout, "Ye gods, Charlotte!" "Ye gods, that looks awful," he once commented on a silver-and-black layered evening dress. "You look like a snake. Doesn't she look like a snake, Dabney?" He used to spout lots of poetry and Shakespeare and make jokes about Grippit Glue, and he suggested that his own money came from a much less dismal source—banking, or railroads, or something like that. In any event, I used to love to watch him clip stock coupons with Charlotte's lethal silver manicure scissors. His favorite expression in those early days was "Oh, bilge!"

Unfortunately alcohol was ever Austin's curse. At first he became exuberant; cheer and goodwill seemed to percolate from his heavy muscular frame. But as time passed (and the drinking became more frequent and prolonged) after the second or third or perhaps the twenty-second or twenty-third drink he would suddenly collapse and vacillate wildly between weeping and bitter denunciations of Belle Haven and everyone in it. Mute Marian was terrified of him after he ambushed her and throttled her one morning as she came out of Charlotte's bedroom carrying a load of dirty sheets for the laundry chute. She bore the marks of his fingers on her neck for weeks.

The summer before my freshman year at Merrywell College, I came to Belle Haven to find Austin was not there. Charlotte said simply that he was sick and in the hospital, and she and Eugene talked in low tones muttering foreign phrases like "non compos mentis," which she explained only meant that Austin was no longer responsible for himself.

The following summer he was back at Belle Haven, but he never again said "Ye gods, Charlotte" or "Oh, bilge." When society women or other luminaries dined at Belle Haven, Austin was decidedly not present and, indeed, the number of grand social functions dwindled to the mandatory Hunt Ball and perhaps one or two others. Austin seldom joined Charlotte and Eugene and me in the dining room and when he did, his hands shook. Invariably he spilled wine all over himself and seemed not to notice. He never left the house, and spent most of his time in his room listening to tinny old songs on the Victrola and drinking. Late one night I was awakened by the sound of his door flung open, the music of the Victrola pouring forth, and Austin's great frame dancing toward Charlotte's room, calling on her to dance with him, begging her in three-quarter time, and then I heard her door burst open and the air filled suddenly with screams—male and female, scurrying, and curses. The following morning I found the Victrola smashed in a thousand pieces on the veranda beneath Austin's window. He then took up with the Bible, continually muttering biblical phrases, often confusing and contorting them unintentionally. One could no longer tell if he was drunk or sober.

The night I returned disgraced from Merrywell, Austin did not join us at dinner. Neither Charlotte nor Eugene remarked on his absence or his afternoon outburst. It did not seem to have upset either of them, but it had severely rattled Favour. He spilled the soup, and a tray of wineglasses chattered in his hands; he tripped on the rug and dropped the cutlery.

"Favour is worse than usual tonight," said Eugene, lifting a delicate pink shrimp to his blue and bloodless lips. (I realized then why Eugene always smiled with his mouth closed; he had bad teeth, which upset the symmetry of his long-jawed face.)

"Yes," Charlotte agreed, "I think he's hopeless. Perhaps I ought to have Marian serve from now on. She's perfect for the task, isn't she? The dumb waiter." Charlotte and Eugene both laughed at her witticism and she tossed another piece of meat to Caesar, who seldom left her side.

Except for James Favour, I thought to myself, nothing had changed at Belle Haven, including Charlotte's sense of humor. The dining room was dreary as ever, though it wasn't supposed to be; it was spacious and well lit with French doors that led out to a small breakfast patio, and a portrait of my grandfather graced the mantel. The painting flattered him: a lyre and palette lay at his feet, and he stood with one hand tucked into his coat, Napoleonic fashion, and the other extended in a gesture of artful generosity. Fittingly, Charlotte now sat in his place at the head of the table, in a gown of butterscotch yellow. To her right sat Eugene in black evening clothes, which gave him the look of a professional mourner.

From where I sat on Charlotte's left I had the full view of a mural painted across the dining-room wall just above the sideboard. It was intended to decorate but, in fact, only served to darken the room. It was a hunting scene, but not one depicting the brilliant October foliage, more the dull gray rag ends of November. Belle Haven crowned the mural's background and riders on beautiful horses—women with their veils flying, men with their crops raised—galloped across the foreground. My grandfather recognizably led the scarlet-and-black–clad riders. In the right-hand corner a pack of dogs cornered a cringing fox; the dogs had drawn blood, but the fox still lived. The bleeding, doomed fox regarded the dogs with implacable hatred, not as if she feared death, but as if the dogs were unworthy of her blood. It was signed *A.D.B. 1899*. My father had painted the mural. When I was a child it had given me nightmares, but I now regarded bloodletting in the dining room simply as bad taste.

"Well, Dabney," Charlotte burst through my thoughts,

"your two years at Merrywell College don't seem to have improved your mind, your clothes, or your social presence."

She sipped her wine and the candlelight caught the topaz of her ring and brooch and the gold in her eyes. "Always the little lady, aren't you, Dabney? The perfect little lady. The well-mannered pumpkin. No more brains than a pumpkin."

"You have to give her some credit for imagination," said Eugene, dabbing his lips with his napkin. "The cow in the library required some imagination and some daring."

"Are you daring and imaginative, Dabney?"

"I don't know."

"The perfect Dabney answer."

I kept my eyes on the white roses in the center of the table as she rang for Favour and said they would take their coffee in the library. I said I was too tired to join them and wanted only to go to bed. Favour left a scarlet stain of wine across the tablecloth as he cleared the glasses.

I did go to bed, got undressed and under the covers, but I did not go to sleep. I lay there in the darkness till I could hear Belle Haven shutting down for the night: the last door closed, the last heart-shaped lock turned, the last toilet flushed, the last of the servants' unobtrusive tread. I waited another hour before I got up, drew on my cotton robe, and made my way quietly, stealthily, down the staircase and into the main salon.

I switched on the light and instantly twenty-four electric candles held in brackets of two burst into unflickering flame and the room—with its matching fireplaces, blue velvet drapes, and carmine Persian carpet—came to life, inasmuch as such a cold room can. The four Beale portraits of the Fairchild beauties were placed two by two over the fireplaces. Charlotte, Francesca, and Alicia had been painted in gowns of seashell pink, sunshine yellow, minty blue against floral backgrounds. Francesca looked lively and impish, blond Ali-

cia as if she might at any minute break into song, and Charlotte—her hair upswept, her shoulders bared—unmistakably
exuded the social presence she so clearly found lacking in
me. The hues of Charlotte's skin were all peach and rose,
and she looked almost succulent.

The portrait of my mother was qualitatively different from
the other three. Julia was painted against a background of
severe shadow, shades of black glinting with bronze high-
lights. Her abundant high-piled hair gleamed with coppery
light and surrounded a face that was serene and glowing. Her
dress, unlike the others', was simple unto starkness. The other
sisters were firmly corseted into their clothes, but Julia's body
seemed fluid and supple beneath the cream-colored satin.
Her arms were round and bare, but a length of chocolate
satin shawl fell from her elbows and melted into the darkness
behind her—as if this vision of light and loveliness had
emerged like dawn out of blackest night.

I often made these midnight pilgrimages to look at her
portrait and as ever I was filled with an immense longing
for her. My father, in truth, meant little to me except
for his unwelcome last name, which I trailed behind me,
a walking reminder of Julia's folly. But my mother was
always very vivid. Sometimes, even now, though she's been
dead for the better part of a century, I hear her voice at
the edge of my sleep. I remembered and I resolved never
to forget her, especially since no one else wanted to remember. It seemed my responsibility to make certain that
Julia Fairchild Beale did not live or die or bear a child in
vain.

And then, as always, I moved from her portrait to gaze
into the diamond-dust–backed mirror. But even its expensive
sparkle could add little luster to my undistinguished face.
Sometimes I aped the expressions of the Fairchild beauties
in the portraits and I thought, perhaps if my mother had

lived, I would have been a great beauty because she would have thought me so.

I turned out the lights in the salon, but lingered, as I always did, hoping that perhaps under cover of darkness, in some insubstantial moment, Julia would whisper to me, that paint and canvas might be animated by the sheer power of my love. I always knew, though, that if she ever deigned to speak, it would not be in the painted presence of the other Fairchild beauties or while Charlotte's vigilant eyes gazed at her across the room.

I closed the door softly and started up the stairs. Experience had taught me there was a particularly hideous squeak on stair ten and another on number fourteen. I skipped those and stuck close to the wall so the balustrade would not groan under my hand. I had never yet been caught on one of my midnight visits to the salon and had no wish to be caught now. At the top of the stairs the long black hall and the landing were quiet and as I started towards my room the darkness behind me seemed to gather with audible breathing and the air grew moist with human sweat. I turned but before I could scream, a hand clapped over my mouth and Eugene Duckworth drew my head into his arms.

"Don't scream," he whispered harshly. "You must promise."

I nodded but he seemed unconvinced. He looked back over his shoulder in the direction of Charlotte's door. "If I take my hand away will you promise not to scream?"

Again I nodded and slowly he withdrew his hand from my mouth, wiping it on his dressing gown. I could see his face more clearly now, his eyes as black as unlit coal and the stiff, clipped nose hairs bristling.

"What are you doing?" he demanded. "Where were you? No, never mind, don't tell me. Just go to bed and stay there. Do you understand?"

I left him without ever speaking. I knew he waited where

he stood until my door was closed and I was safely in bed. Finally I heard the door to his room whisper shut and it was only then that I realized that if he had let me answer his question, I would certainly have had the right to ask him where he was going and what he was doing at that late, lonely hour.

3

Charlotte always took her breakfast in bed on a tray and Austin kept no schedule; he rose, slept, ate, and of course drank at whim. So only Eugene was on the breakfast patio the next morning when I came down. He made no mention of our nocturnal encounter; indeed he studied the morning papers, quite oblivious to me. "I'm finished, Favour, but I'll have more coffee," he said to the flaxen-haired butler, who lingered just inside the dining-room door.

Favour poured us each some coffee, spilling mine into the saucer. "That's all right," I said reassuringly, but when I looked at him, his eyes were empty and cloudless as the May morning sky.

Eugene told Favour to leave the silver coffeepot there on the table and when Favour had retreated, Eugene looked at me for the first time. "What do you think of Favour, Dabney?"

"I think he's very clumsy and I can't imagine why Charlotte puts up with him."

"He's beautiful, of course. One tolerates a good deal for beauty."

I said nothing. I didn't quite understand what he was getting at.

He lit a cigarette. "Belle Haven is a suitable frame for such beauty, not only Favour's, but Charlotte's. It doesn't suit you, Dabney. Not in the least and I hope you don't cherish any misguided notions of inheriting it one day. Ah, you look at me surprised, as though such a thought had never crossed your virginal little mind. You are still a virgin, aren't you?" He paused as though he actually expected me to answer. I drank my coffee, ignoring the intimacy he seemed not simply to foster but to insist upon. His very tone rang with insinuation. "Belle Haven is the perfect frame for the grace and beauty that money can buy. Money can buy anything." Smoke billowed from his nostrils. "Almost anything."

"I'm surprised to hear you say 'almost,' Eugene," I declared breezily. He seemed to be set upon some nasty game of wits and even if I was not his equal, I knew better than to cower.

"There are some things only time can buy. Breeding, for instance. It takes three generations to make a gentleman. Four to make a lady. Charles Fairchild—give him credit—knew that. He knew and he didn't give a damn. He wanted to do it all in a matter of years and I suppose he succeeded. At least by some standard. He certainly had lots of money and that helps. He had me."

"You?"

Eugene crushed out his butt in a crystal ashtray. "Why do you think Charles Fairchild hired me? Isn't Virginia full of lawyers? Why do you think I, in particular, was chosen?"

I said I didn't know, but in truth, it would never have occurred to me to ask. Eugene Duckworth was like part of the furniture. I would have sooner inquired after the origins of the chair I sat on.

"I lent Charles Fairchild a kind of luster he could not otherwise have had. Ever. My family was once as grand as this. Grander. To employ a Duckworth as a lawyer, a sort of coolie, bent double, slaving in his legal fields. What more could a Fairchild ask for?"

Naturally I did not know. Moreover, I could not imagine Eugene Duckworth bent double over anything. "You are a lawyer, aren't you? You do legal things."

"Yes. Everything I do is legal." He grinned and showed his bad teeth. "But you honestly mean to tell me, you've never heard of the Duckworths? No. I can see by the ignorance all over your plain face you haven't. You've never heard of George Mason or Carter Burwell either, have you? Great Virginia names. My ancestors were their peers, their comrades, their schoolmates. The names mean nothing?" He laughed with his old corrosiveness. "Of course not. They don't teach real history at Merrywell, do they? It behooves the papas of Merrywell girls to keep them ignorant of the past. So that the little dewdrop daughters will know nothing of the past. Nothing at all." He lingered over these words as though he had salted and cured them. "They do not want their little simpering dewdrops to know the truth of human intercourse—I use the word advisedly, Dabney—which is to say what motivates, dictates human intercourse. The past. Of course. Not lust. Not greed, though I do not discount lust and greed." He raised a hairy eyebrow. "But they are fleeting and easily assuaged. The past, on the other hand, is remorseless. To exonerate, or conceal, or avenge the past, why, that can absorb your whole life, long after lust has lost its appeal and greed its pleasures. Or, perhaps it's the other way around. Lust has its pleasures and greed its appeal. What do you think, Dabney? How would you phrase it?"

"I don't know," I said brusquely.

"Think about it."

I wanted to evaporate on the spot, but he held me seemingly riveted with those cold narrow eyes. He poured me some more coffee with a gesture almost gallant and, so, all the more unsettling.

"The fact that you are here in this beautiful house on this beautiful spring morning testifies to lust and greed—your mother's lust and your father's greed." He held up a hand to silence me even before I could leap to my parents' defense. "I'm describing a situation, Dabney, not commenting on their morals. I have no interest in morals. None whatever. No interest in passion or anger or anything of that sort. It's dangerous. In fact, your parents had run off to England before I ever came to Belle Haven, so I only know of their story by hearsay. But they seem to have been ruled by passion." He lit another cigarette. "However, passion hardly looks to have passed on to you, a dismal child. Will you grow from a dismal child into a dull woman? I wonder. Will you actually be attractive one day?" His eyes roved over me. Up and down. "Drink your coffee. I poured it for you."

I did as I was bid. Despite the warm spring morning, last night's creeping fear came over me.

He smoked expansively. "Well, allow me to correct Merrywell's oversight, Dabney. The Duckworths were a most illustrious family. They were an illustrious family when the Fairchilds were still grubbing roots. Alas, the War—and by that I do not mean the late, lamented conflict with Europe, but the only war worth talking about, the War Between the States—that war brought my family's power and ascendancy to an end. I was born into the rag ends of all that. I tasted none of it. The generation before me, the Duckworths lost everything. Land. Houses. Money. Everything, my parents were fond of saying, except our honor. And that followed in short order, because when you do not have property or money, your honor is not worth a damn. You look bored, Dabney. History too much for you?"

"Not bored, exactly," I said, "but this is a story I've heard before."

"Indeed? Where?"

"Everybody at Merrywell had a story something like that. The Lost Plantation Story." I rolled my eyes. I couldn't help it. "I know it well."

"They're all liars," he said, clearly more vehemently than he wished, because he immediately settled back with his cigarette. "You see, Dabney, if they were telling the truth, they could not have afforded to go to Merrywell College. The only girls who could afford Merrywell are all the daughters of plutocrats and carpetbaggers like your late esteemed grandfather. Oh, the occasional charity girl, of course. The charity girls might actually have been telling the truth. The Lost Plantation Story." He mimicked my intonation brutally. "The rest of them tell their children that story to dignify the ugly way they came into their money. Charlotte says she doesn't give a damn for the dignity of her money, but she doesn't exactly like to talk about Grippit Glue, either." He gave a low, mean chuckle as though the thought of Grippit filled him with glee. "But she's a remarkable woman in any event. Rich. Beautiful. Ruthless. Heartless. Truly, she has no heart. That's the fundamental error her husbands have made. That all her husbands will make."

"All her husbands?"

Eugene called for Favour and told him to have his car brought round. "Charlotte will always have a husband," he continued. "She needs one. Husbands have a convenient way of giving a woman like Charlotte respectability. Even her money couldn't do that. Not by itself. And, as soon as Austin drinks himself into the grave—which looks as though it will be soon—Charlotte will marry again."

"Will she marry you, Eugene?" I asked with a nasty sort of bravado. I surprised myself.

But I did not seem to surprise Eugene. He laughed. "Do I look stupid? Only a very stupid man would marry Charlotte. She destroys men in general, but husbands in particular. Look what happened to that first one, Doctor what's-his-name. And one need not have a great mind to see what Austin has become. No, I pity the men who love Charlotte, and though such men deserve what they get, still I would pity them. But,

more than that"—Eugene rose and put out his cigarette—
"God pity the man Charlotte loves. If she can. If she's capable
of love, which is dubious. But if she is, God pity the poor
sod." Favour came in to say his car would be in front shortly.
Eugene did not so much as thank him. "Go get my briefcase
from the library. Put it in the front hall and leave it there."

Favour vanished and then Eugene did a very odd thing.
He took my chin in his hand. His skin was dry and coarse
and the hand itself was bony. Yet his touch was not unkind,
which unnerved me. I felt queasy. "Perhaps someone ought
to remind your aunt that you are a grown woman now and
not a little girl." His fingers tightened on my jaws till they
hurt. "I'm going to give you some free advice, Dabney. Don't
wander about Belle Haven at night. Your Uncle Austin is
not a well man. There's no telling what he might do if he
were provoked or frightened." Eugene moved his fingers
slowly up my cheeks and pressed so hard my lips were forced
to pucker for him. He brought his face very close to mine,
so close I could smell the cigarette on his breath. "You understand, Dabney? The next time, it might cost you dearly."

I sat where I was till I heard his feet cross the front hall,
heard the front door close and the sound of his tires on the
gravel. I would not risk meeting Eugene alone even in broad
daylight, much less the night. But as soon as I knew he was
gone, I bolted straight from the breakfast patio and ran for
the lake, for the clean serenity and solitude of the lake.

There was no direct path. I had to follow the boxwood
maze through a series of tiny courtyards, some with fountains,
some with fish ponds, all with classical statuary. A sculptor
was once one of my grandfather's beneficiaries, but none of
the sculpture was very original—lots of classically draped
nymphs, some holding bunches of grapes above their gaping
mouths, some stroking lyres with their stone fingers, a Diana
armed for the hunt. Most interesting—and disturbing—was

a statue of a small fat cherub with his hands bound behind his back, tied with a thorny rose garland. I could not tell if his face was contorted in pleasure or pain.

Past the formal gardens I went through a makeshift gate where the path sloped down a gentle hill, growing narrower by the minute. Perhaps the path was discernible only to me, since I was the one who had made it. It led through the trees and over a small muddy stream to the Belle Haven Lake.

Since my last visit the winter before, one of the docks had rotted completely and part of the boathouse roof had caved in. I could tell that, when summer came, vines would overtake the boathouse altogether. A chorus of birds sounded from inside its rafters. The tender, tentative green of April had faded from the surrounding hillsides and the more robust foliage of May had taken its place. My arrival startled a family of ducks, who screamed and flew to the opposite shore, leaving ever-widening ripples across the water's surface. I gathered some stones from the bank and walked out to the edge of the diving board, where I swung my feet and tossed the stones. The morning sun warmed my back and I welcomed it after my conversation with Eugene Duckworth.

The three rowboats—the *Charlotte, Francesca,* and *Alicia*—were not maintained. Indeed, I suspect no one had so much as approached this lake in the months I'd been gone. Rainwater and clotted, decaying leaves and blossoms—the residue of passing seasons—putrefied in the bottom of the boats. I found the boathouse key exactly where I'd left it, beneath a damp board. I brushed off the slugs and put it in the heart-shaped lock, which groaned and gave way. The boathouse had also served as a bathhouse and was divided into several small rooms used for changing. I never left my own bathing costume or towel there because it was dim, damp, and cobwebbed and things rotted quickly. Four sets of oars were still neatly bracketed on the walls and several coils of rope hung in their accustomed place.

I took the rope, a few rags, and a small whisk broom and began with the *Alicia,* untying it from the remaining dock and towing it to shore, where I began cleaning. I vowed every year that I would paint the three little boats, but I never did. Not because I was too lazy to paint—I would have enjoyed it; in fact I had even toyed with the idea of fixing up the boathouse so it would be almost habitable, but I was reluctant to ask Charlotte for the money for materials: I did not want her—or anyone else—to know where or how I spent so much of my time. I was more or less invisible at Belle Haven and I liked it that way. Charlotte clearly liked it that way too. She never once asked where I was and I never once offered to tell her.

The boats were in worse shape than I'd guessed, but I did what I could that morning with the *Alicia* and returned to the house for lunch when the sun was high overhead.

To my surprise, Charlotte did not mention the cow, my expulsion from Merrywell, or any of my other numerous defects. Instead, she complained about her hairdresser's marrying and leaving Oakstone and described in her witty and acerbic way the shortcomings of the ladies on the Cultural League Steering Committee and the Heritage Foundation Governing Board and the stupidity of her bridge partner at the last Assistance League luncheon. She waxed on at great length about a recent letter from Francesca, who was living in London and anxious to marry yet again; this time the prospective groom was a lower-rung noble with (she assured Charlotte) plenty of money. The main obstacle in the path of Francesca's true happiness was the noble's inconvenient wife. Divorce in England was tedious and expensive.

It was actually rather pleasant to sit on the patio, sip white wine, and listen to Charlotte. She had a rich, moist voice— husky, sometimes so monotonous that I forgot what she was saying and heard only the cadences. Besides, I wasn't used to having wine in the middle of the day and the second glass and the surrounding sunshine dulled me unto sleep. I nodded affirmatively when Charlotte required it, but for the most part I concentrated simply on her voice and the begonias flowering in their pot on the lunch table. I did not realize until jolted awake when Favour interrupted us that their tangerine color precisely matched the long silk scarf wound around Charlotte's neck, heightening her cheek color and giving her an artificial but effective glow.

"Excuse me, madame," said Favour, "but there's a young man to see you."

"A young man? What's his name?"

"He would not give his name, madame, he only said he wished to see you."

"Well, send him in, Favour. I never keep young men waiting."

A slow blush spread over Favour's cheeks. At least, I thought, he's got blood in his veins instead of the milk his pallor suggested. He left us and returned with a man who stood in brilliant contrast to the pale Favour. He had abundant dark hair and a tanned, even-featured face. He was bearded, which was not at all common in those days, and the beard made him look serious and sturdy. Standing side by side the two men reminded me of a strong earthenware vessel beside a pale porcelain plate.

"The young man, madame," said Favour ineptly.

"I can see that."

The man's hazel eyes—neither quite brown nor quite green—rested briefly on me and then turned to Charlotte, who recrossed her legs and held her wineglass as if it were a long-stemmed rose. Favour withdrew, tripping at the edge of the patio. "I take it you know who I am," said Charlotte in her most cultivated tone, "but I'm sure I haven't the pleasure of your acquaintance."

"We're acquainted, in a manner of speaking. You might even say we're related."

"Really? How interesting. I hope you're not a poor relation here to beg."

"I never beg."

"I thought not."

I thought not too; the man was hatless and poised and he did not so much as glance around him, unlike most visitors to Belle Haven, who often grew wide-eyed and inarticulate at its splendor.

"Which branch of the family did you spring from, Mr.—"

"The Hamilton branch. I'm William Bayard Hamilton the Third. You were married to my father."

This seemed a preposterous statement to me, at least on the face of it, and as I tried to rouse myself from the wine-inflicted torpor, I noted that Charlotte's grip on her wineglass had tightened, but other than that she evinced no emotion whatever.

"Well, Mr. Hamilton, what can I—"

"Dr. Hamilton."

"Doctor! Following in your father's footsteps, are you? Admirable."

I tried to reconstruct the face of the Doctor, Charlotte's husband when I first came to Belle Haven, but he was a shadowy, lost figure. I remembered his vaguely gingery smell—a combination of cigar smoke and antiseptic—and remembered that he once made a house call on my ailing doll, but other than that, he receded to the dim pall of the past. His son, however, was anything but dim. He stood like a lightning rod, crackling in the spring-soft afternoon. I'd never known the Doctor had a son; indeed, I realized at that moment I'd never known anything about him, not even his first name.

"What can I do for you, Doctor? Would you like to have

a look at my tonsils?" Charlotte licked her lips and for one moment I thought she might actually open her mouth for his inspection. "Will you take a seat or do you prefer to stand about like a servant?"

Young Dr. Hamilton took a seat between us and I hoped Charlotte would introduce us, but she didn't. "Will you have a glass of wine, Dr. Hamilton? No? Just like your father, aren't you? Never drink during the day."

"I did not come here to drink. I came to collect my father's things."

"His what?"

"His things. I came to collect the things he left at Belle Haven."

"And what might those be?" Charlotte flipped open her gold cigarette case and nonchalantly tapped a cigarette.

"I'm not sure. I only know that when he died he left a great many things at Belle Haven and I'd like them given to my mother. They cannot matter to you and they would mean a great deal to her."

"Still the suffering saint, your mother? Didn't she ever remarry?"

"No, she never did."

"Dedicated her life to her son, is that it? A suffering insufferable saint, your mother." The words billowed out on a banner of smoke. "Just like your father, Dr. Hamilton, and doubtless just like you. You come from a family of sanctimonious prigs." She snapped her fingers and Caesar trotted over to be patted on the head.

Dr. Hamilton folded his strong capable-looking hands on the table. "I don't see how you can say that," he replied evenly. "After all, my father wasn't such a prig. He slept with you, didn't he, committed adultery with you, and in fact he did better—or worse—than that. He left his wife and child to live with you, and divorced so that he could make an honest woman of you, if such a thing is possible, which I doubt. He

was every bit as much a sinner as you, Mrs. Courtney, but"—
the young doctor shrugged, regarding Charlotte coolly—"my
father paid for his sins. Have you?"

Charlotte pursed her lips momentarily around the cigarette
and left a bright tangerine stain there before blowing her
smoke into Dr. Hamilton's eyes. "So you're a moralist as well
as a doctor. Two can play at morals, you know, and it's my
opinion that suicide is not so much paying for your sins as
obliterating them."

I nearly fell into the remains of my crab salad. No one had
ever told me the Doctor had committed suicide. I kept my
eyes on the young Dr. Hamilton's hands, half afraid he would
smash the wineglasses, scatter the begonias.

"You're hardly in a position to moralize, Mrs. Courtney.
Waxing philosophic is unbecoming to you."

"And impertinence is unbecoming to you."

Dr. Hamilton cleared his throat. "I did not come here to
quarrel, only to ask for my father's things back."

"I threw everything of William's away when he died."

"I don't believe that. Not even you would have thrown
away a man's suicide note."

"What makes you think he left a note?"

"My father was a methodical man, Mrs. Courtney. He even
committed suicide in a methodical way. He slit his wrists with
his own scalpel and got into a tub of warm water. My father
kept meticulous medical records. He would not have committed the ultimate surgery without leaving a note."

Charlotte listened to all this calmly, as if she were actually
interested in his assessment. She put out her cigarette, though
blue smoke hovered over the table like a wraith. "Your father's been dead seven years. Why didn't you come around
then?"

"I was only eighteen then and besides I'm not asking for
myself. Nothing can bring my father back to life and nothing
can undo the damage he wreaked. I'm here for my mother.

My mother is dying of cancer and she would very much like to have my father's things. And, as you point out, Mrs. Courtney, he's been dead seven years, you've remarried, I can't see what difference it would make to you, and it would mean a great deal to her. It's all in the past—a dead man, a dying woman, what can it matter?" He spoke as if we the living were somehow segregated and allied against the dead and dying. Yet, I could tell he felt very deeply for his mother. I was moved and hoped Charlotte would be too.

"You're quite right, Doctor. It doesn't matter anymore."

I was actually proud of my aunt in that moment; her beauty seemed heightened by dignity.

"Then may I come to collect my father's things at some convenient time?"

"There is no convenient time. There never will be. I am your father's widow and whatever he left is by rights mine and I'll never give it up."

"I'm ready to pay if you like."

"Pay! You want to buy moldy anatomy books and prescription blanks and records on the rickety undernourished bodies of his poor stinking patients; you might recall that only the poorest trash in this county—white, black, green, or blue—would call on your father's professional services after he came to Belle Haven—and then only because he'd quit charging. He didn't need the money anymore, you see. He had me."

"My guess, Mrs. Courtney, is that you had him."

"You make me laugh!" And indeed she did laugh—the old Charlotte, all parry and thrust, but if she expected him to crumble under her scorn, she was wrong.

"You may keep my father's anatomy books and prescription blanks. All I want is the suicide note."

"You are a sentimental fool, Dr. Hamilton. Your father was a sentimental fool and your mother is a sentimental fool. The answer is no."

"I had hoped you'd see it my way."

"Oh, I do. I'm sorry your mother's dying, at least I think I am. It's difficult to muster any sympathy for a cringing, sanctimonious, nerveless stranger, but if you expected to come here and use your dying mother to bludgeon a little guilt into me, then you've wasted your time."

"My mother is no longer bitter, Mrs. Courtney. She's long since let go of her bitterness."

"The more fool she. And you, Dr. Hamilton? The little lost orphan whose nasty daddy ran off with a rich woman—are you bitter? Would you like it better if your nasty daddy had run off with a poor woman? Would that make it nicer and easier to bear?"

Under his beard I could see Dr. Hamilton's lips were pressed into a tight seam, though when he spoke his voice was cool and professional. "I am committed to healing when I can, to easing suffering when I can, and it is in this spirit only that I ask you for my father's things. I do not live in the past. It does not matter to me."

"That's all very noble, Doctor, wonderfully said, but nobility bores me. It puts me in a perfect coma of boredom and so if you really want to ease someone's suffering, you'll ease mine and get to hell out of my house."

As Dr. Hamilton rose, his chair scraped the flagstones with a jarring dull shriek. "This isn't the end of this matter, Mrs. Courtney. I'll take it to court if necessary. I'm sure that Charlotte Courtney wouldn't want to stand up in court and—"

"I never stand up in court, Doctor. I never go to court. You may do what you like, but don't waste my time with your ridiculous threats. I have been sued by experts. That's why I have an expert lawyer and if you want to waste Eugene Duckworth's time, it will cost you money. Do whatever you damn please, only get out of Belle Haven."

As he stood before us, William Bayard Hamilton III gave me a cold, complicated glance. "Miss," he said curtly. Turning back to Charlotte, he reached into his pocket and left his card, with an Oakstone address, on the table. "This is in case you change your mind."

"Get out."

After he left Charlotte tore his card to shreds and let them fall like petals into her wineglass. She left the patio, giving Caesar an unexplained kick.

We ebbed into summer carelessly, and the tumult of spring receded into the past. I spent the lengthening days at the lake. I finally cleaned up all three boats, even secretly invested in some paint (I got the money from Austin during one of his weak moments and went one Thursday into Oakstone with Ethel, the cook, to get supplies). I painted them all a jaunty yellow, my favorite color (perhaps because I'm too sallow to wear it). The three sanded, painted, refurbished boats stood in glorious contrast to the weathered green boards of the crumbling dock and the broken roof of the boathouse. I considered expending some effort on the boathouse too, but it was summer, after all, time to swim, read, float, and play the flute, not sweat and steam under the hot eaves of the boathouse, which nature clearly intended to reclaim no matter what I did.

That summer Charlotte convened frequently with other wealthy clubwomen like herself and attended meetings, luncheons, and bridge parties. She even hosted a Fourth of July picnic around the swimming pool for anyone (of sufficient social status) who was fool enough to be in Virginia in midsummer. Charlotte invested this party with her usual style, complete with fireworks and an orchestra and a massive red, white, and blue cake. The first guests to arrive, I might add, were the family doctor and his wife. Dr. Pruitt sedated Austin so he would not present a potential problem during the party. The doctor—who, I suspect, was amply rewarded for his ministrations to the ailing Austin—also brought with him a black male nurse to sit with Austin in the event he should waken. Before the party Charlotte inspected my dress and hair and shoes. She approved without enthusiasm and admonished me to dance with the young men, to avoid all mention of the cow episode, and to be agreeable and socially pleasant, if that was possible. "It distresses me," she concluded, "when you look like a fool."

I had little opportunity to disgrace her. For most of the party I was the virtual prisoner of a fat balding gent who regaled me with stories of my Aunt Alicia's loveliness and how he had courted her in the old days.

But save for that midsummer party, those of us who lived at Belle Haven generally met only in the evenings. During the day Charlotte rode her roan mare, Dancer, with Caesar at her heels. She swam or played tennis with Eugene, who came over three times a week and spent every weekend there as well. After dinner Eugene and Charlotte closeted themselves to discuss business. Doubtless they remained together through the night in my aunt's bed, but I never again met Eugene on the stairs, because I took his advice and did not prowl Belle Haven at night. I might have put a cow in the library, but I would not court danger for its own sake.

As for Austin, he got better and then worse and for a time would eat nothing but loaves and fishes till he tired of that diet. One night he joined us in the dining room. No one remarked on his presence or the peculiar look on his face. Then, to my horror, he devoured nearly a whole sirloin of beef. Even Caesar's gaze was riveted on Austin. Unwillingly my eyes went to the mural of the dogs gnawing into the succulent red flesh of the fox and from there to Austin, his teeth gnashing, the small red pool of blood and juice collecting in his plate, his greasy chin. I asked to be excused.

"Ignore him, Dabney," Charlotte said blithely. "Austin is trying to drive us all from the table, aren't you, Austin?"

Austin hunkered over his plate. "God knows everything," he replied. "God knows what you've done and what you are. No sin escapes God's eyes."

"What does God think of drunkenness, Austin? Perhaps God would like me better if I kept the liquor from you. I'm breaking the law for you, Austin, Prohibition and all that. Maybe I should lock up the liquor."

"Some sins are worse than others," said Austin in a remarkable fit of lucidity. His jaws worked over a hunk of meat. "If you want to know about sin, ask the moneychanger over there." He wagged a thick finger toward Eugene. "Ask that pharisee. Ask that blight on God's eye."

Eugene went gray about the gills, but Charlotte did not so much as flinch.

"Ask the whoremonger," Austin continued, "God's got no mercy for the unregenerate, the unredeemed. The whores and their pimps will burn in hell. Thou whore," he said directly to Charlotte. "Thou pimp," to Eugene.

A perceptible tension flickered over Charlotte's well-boned face, but she kept eating daintily and remarked in passing that if Austin did not shut up she would have no choice but to think him utterly mad and commit him once again to the hospital.

Austin collapsed in front of our eyes; his great frame slid gelatinously to the floor and he gasped, gurgled, near to vomiting all the beef he'd ingested.

"Favour," said Charlotte peremptorily, "help Mr. Courtney to his room."

"I—I can't, madame."

"And why not?"

"He's too big."

"You'll do as you're told, Favour."

Favour, grunting and panting under the strain, raised the stricken Austin from the floor and supported him out of the room.

"Pass the salt, Dabney," said Charlotte.

Now and then Charlotte addressed herself to "Dabney's Problem"—that is, what was to be done with me. She asked if I wanted to visit Francesca in London, but I begged off. Francesca was the most highly strung of all my aunts and the thought of her "sick headaches" and her troubles with her married lover did not appeal to me. Charlotte at least was predictable; she never suffered from sick headaches and whatever difficulties she may have had with her lover, Eugene Duckworth, she kept them to herself. Finally, she announced that when Alicia returned from her round-the-world cruise in the fall she'd discuss my fate with Alicia. That was the last heard of "Dabney's Problem."

This indefinite solution was fine with me. After all, I was simply serving out the term of my youth until the day I was twenty-one, when I would no longer be anyone's ward and would come into my mother's share of my grandfather's legacy. Francesca once told me this comforting bit of information and then she immediately made me promise not to tell Charlotte. It was supposed to be a surprise and she said that Charlotte got very angry when her surprises were spoiled.

So I was content to remain at Belle Haven, sheltered, indulged, or at least ignored, practicing the piano (when Charlotte was out of the house; for all my lessons, she said I played the piano like I was operating a linen press) and being sole proprietor of the Lake Domain, floating aimlessly while I waited for the currents of time to take me to the age of twenty-one. Time is inexorable, I've since learned, and relentless, and on July 21, 1921, my frail ark of complacency was forever shattered and I was swept into a current that propelled me back into the past as well as towards the future.

It had been insufferably hot all week, the humidity unendurable, and the night brought no relief. I slept and woke and slept and woke to find perspiration gathered in small lakes at my neck and knees. I kicked off the sheet and lay in my thin cotton nightdress, sweating, sleepless, dreamless as only the young can be. I got up and walked to the window, where the cool moonlight belied the steamy night and not so much as a breeze ruffled the leafy underskirts of the trees. The house seemed to hold the heat in its very fist, and on impulse I gathered up my shoes and decided to make for the lake, defying Eugene's advice. Once when I was fourteen, I had gone to the lake in the middle of the night, taken out a boat, and fallen asleep in it. I didn't wake till the sun was high in the sky and I could hear the servants and dogs searching the woods for me. When they brought me before Charlotte she sentenced me to two days in my room, solitary meals, and no books or games (though Austin smuggled me a couple of H. G. Wells's novels). Still, I reflected, stealthily opening my door and peering into the empty hall, I was not a child anymore and I doubted very much if Charlotte cared where I slept.

Carrying my shoes, I closed my door without so much as a click and surveyed the hall carefully. I could have used the servants' stairway, which was closer, but the door had a dreadful squeal. I would have to brave a couple of empty guest rooms and bathrooms, Austin's room, and Eugene's room. I felt confident that Austin had passed out and that Eugene would be with Charlotte; with stealth and impunity, I could surely cross the landing.

As I tiptoed across the hall, however, I wondered if I had misjudged Austin. Weeping, audible, pained whimpering floated across the hall. I pressed my ear to Austin's door, but only his bellowing, inebriated snores echoed. It was not Austin. No, the sobs came from Charlotte's room.

I should have gone on or gone back, raced for the safety of my room, the safety of ignorance, but the awful weeping touched a cord within me and I very carefully moved towards Charlotte's door. I could not imagine Charlotte Courtney with so much as a single tear marring her face, much less this plaintive whimpering. I pressed my ear to the door. It certainly wasn't Charlotte. Nor Eugene. In fact, it sounded neither masculine nor feminine, more childlike, wretched, and neutral. I crouched next to the wall like a curious criminal.

"Get me a cigarette, Eugene," said Charlotte over the damp, heaving sobs. "Really," she added more sharply, "you must stop this."

"Please, madame," mewed the voice, "please don't make me."

"I've told you not to call me madame here. We're Charlotte and Eugene and James here. We're very democratic in this room, aren't we, Eugene?"

"Democratic to a fault."

James? James Favour? Great God in the morning! Despite the heat, my teeth chattered and I nearly began to drip and blubber myself. I stood rooted, transfixed.

"Please Charlotte, please. I told you I'd do anything but that."

"No, James, I don't think you did. I think you agreed to do anything I asked you. Isn't that right, Eugene? When we rescued poor James from that nasty New York brothel, didn't he agree to do anything we asked?"

"That's what he said."

"I will! I will! Only not that, please don't make me."

"Oh blow your nose, James."

He obeyed. "Please, mad—Charlotte. I'll do anything else. I always have, haven't I? Please, Mr. Duck—Eugene, tell her

I've done whatever she wanted, what both of you wanted, but not this."

"You've done it before," said Eugene coolly.

Favour broke into fresh weeping. "Only when I had to."

"You're my servant, James," Charlotte commanded. "You'll do as I say. The faithful servant does as he's told and doesn't ask questions."

"Or make excuses," Eugene added.

"Pour James some more champagne, Eugene. That should help. Drink up, James."

"Please"—his voice rose into a piercing lament.

"Now, that's better isn't it? Now, Eugene, bring me the ice bucket. I think it's just too hot in here. Isn't it, James? James needs to cool off. Come here and lie down. It's the heat that's making you nervous and upset. Come, James."

His feet dragged across the floor and I could hear water sloshing in the ice bucket and then Charlotte's lowest, richest, and most seductive voice reached me, even over Eugene's snickers.

"That's right, James, lie down. I'm going to cool you off. Don't tense up. The ice feels good, doesn't it? Just relax and you'll enjoy it."

"No! No!"

"Do as I say. Just obey me and it will be easy. I'm your mistress, remember James? How can you forget that?" He began to whimper again in irregular sobs, but Charlotte continued. "Have we ever hurt you? No, of course not. We're not going to hurt you. Tell him it doesn't hurt, Eugene."

"He knows what it feels like," Eugene snapped.

"Tell him it doesn't hurt."

"It doesn't hurt, James."

"We'd never hurt you. I'm your mistress and Eugene is your master and I think you're being very faithless and ungrateful. We can't leave Eugene out of our fun, can we? All we want is for you to—"

"No! No!" James's feet thudded across the floor and his heaving breath was audible from where I stood.

"Get out of that corner and get back on this bed. Bring him over here, Eugene."

There was a struggle and Eugene cursed James for being weak-minded and ungrateful and James began to howl, the low bellow of an animal in pain. "Shut up, you fool, you stupid fool," Charlotte said. "You'll wake Austin and the Ugly Duckling. Now come here—you want to lie on the floor? Is it more comfortable for you on the floor?"

"No! No, please."

"Shall I sit on you to hold you down? You can't relax that way, can you? It will be easier if you relax. Get him on the bed, Eugene." And then flesh hit flesh in a bright hard slap and Favour's howls turned to whimpers as the slaps sounded again, three times, four times. Then Charlotte crooned, "You might like it."

"Pl—ease, I'll do anything else you like. I always have."

"You'll do this, too, you retarded little ingrate."

"Oh, forget it, Charlotte," Eugene said wearily. "I'm not in the mood."

"Don't be tiresome, Eugene. It's a matter of principle now, isn't it, James? If James doesn't do as we ask, he'll be disobedient, won't he? And he doesn't want to do that because he knows what happens to unfaithful servants."

"Maybe he doesn't know," said Eugene. "Maybe that's why he's disobedient."

"Do you think that's it?" Charlotte sounded mildly surprised. "You may be right. James only knows what happens to faithful servants. How many servants are treated as you are, James? Hmmm? How many servants have a master in their mistress? Lie down, that's right, that's the way I like to see you, James, yes, compliant and accessible, yes, like that. How many other servants get this from their mistresses?"

A groan sounded from the bed, a deep, exhausted groan, as if it had been pumped from the very core of Favour's being. Nausea overcame me, my stomach churned, my mouth and eyes watered. I clutched my shoes.

"Faithful servants get that, James. Unfaithful servants get the sack. They get thrown out and what do you think happens to them then?"

"They go back to where they came from," Eugene said. "Whatever gutter they crawled out of is always happy to have them back."

"Maybe you'd like to go back, James."

"I'd rather die. I'll do anything."

"Then you'll do as we ask."

"Yes." He crumpled into abject weeping. "Yes, yes. Only—"

"What now? I'm getting very sick of all this."

"Only I need another drink. Please, Charlotte, one more drink and then anything you want, I'll do."

"We're out of champagne," said Eugene.

"Please, Charlotte," Favour wailed.

"Oh, very well, Eugene, put on your clothes and go get some more champagne and I'll stay here and get James back in the mood. We can't have any fun if you're not in the mood, can we, James?"

Rooted to the floor with revulsion, I snapped to attention when I heard the belt buckle on Eugene's pants ringing and the sound of his feet coming towards the door. No escape. I couldn't get down the stairs that fast. My own room was at the other end of the hall. I started to dash for one of the bathrooms when Charlotte's door opened and a patch of light fell into the hall. "Bring some ice while you're at it, Eugene."

"I'm not the servant," he retorted.

Then I saw the laundry chute. Right beside me, beckoning as if its great maw were muttering "Escape, escape." I pulled open the chute and dove in head first, eyes shut; it closed dully behind me and swallowed me up silently as the sea itself.

My descent was swift and uncomplicated and I landed with a thud in a huge bin of dirty clothes in the laundry room in the basement. I stayed where I was because I knew the wine cellar was right beside the laundry room and I could hear Eugene fumbling with the lock, cursing, and finally clinking amongst the bottles of precious bootleg stash. Then I heard the lock turn again and his footsteps retreat. Still, I did not move. I stayed there for what seemed like hours, my eyes gradually becoming accustomed to the darkness and the gray, moonlit shadows cast through the basement's grilled windows. Only when I realized I was lying on top of sheets that came from Belle Haven beds, did I scramble out of the laundry bin, stubbing my toe violently on one of the nearby linen presses.

In the half light I appeared to have stumbled into a torture chamber: the wringer washing machines stood like stout-armed, enameled guards, their huge rollers eager to devour fingers and toes. Heavy black irons lined up like artillery on the shelves above me and the ironing boards resembled rickety prison cots. In the long tunnel before me stretched clotheslines where a few shirts still hung limply like hanging bodies left to rot on gibbets. In the oppressive heat the shirts were sticky and pressed against my perspiring arms like dead men's hands as I made my way through the narrow room, towards some sickly light. There was a grille overhead, no roof, only barred window and sky. If the grille isn't locked, I said to myself as I cautiously came closer, I'm free. If it is locked—but I didn't pursue the thought. I found an old chair at the end of the tunnel, stood on it, and pushed hard on the grille. It creaked ominously, but it opened. The chair was too low to allow me to jump out, but I thought the shelf

beside me might suffice. The shelves held soap and bleach
and cleaning fluids, brushes and washboards. From the chair
I clambered up, praying the shelf would support my weight,
and then I lunged for the opening and pulled my body
through, though my swinging feet caught one of the bottles
on the shelf and it crashed to the floor. Once out, I looked
back down into the hole I'd escaped from and saw lye spread-
ing across the floor. DANGER was writ large across the broken
bottle and a skull and crossbones underlined the warning.
And as I took off running, it seemed to me that the death's
head opened its mouth; laughter pealed forth and chased me
through the boxwood gardens, past the gate, and down the
path through the woods. Unnatural laughter. Like Eugene's.

5

I can't imagine that I slept, but I must have, because I awoke with the just-risen sun beating down on the back of my neck, cramped, sweating, curled up in the *Francesca,* bobbing in the middle of the Belle Haven Lake. I rolled over and the boat's ribs pierced my back. I ran my hands over my face and tried to open my eyes, but the light was too bright. For one last innocent moment I could not remember how or why I'd gone there, but then, unaided, memory spoke and I heard Charlotte's cool demanding voice and Favour's whimpering sobs.

I was nauseated all over again, but the feeling passed. I'd already vomited behind the boathouse the night before. Alas, the mind cannot vomit; no purges are possible for what one can and must remember. The sun penetrated my thin cotton nightdress, warming my flesh, though the marrow of my bones remained chilled as ice.

The unfamiliar yelping of a dog sounded nearby, and as I slowly opened my eyes I thought perhaps they'd unleashed Caesar on me, but it was too early for anyone to have missed me. The barking became more excited and I knew it was not Caesar. Slowly I sat up and brought my eyes to the level of the rim of the boat. A small brown-and-white mutt danced at the edge of the lake, yapping its lungs out. He spied me and barked all the louder. A saddled gray horse, the color of newsprint, stood contented and untethered nearby, nibbling at the tender shoots of grass. In the water, maybe twenty yards from me, something splashed—an arm rose out of the water, paused, and disappeared again into the depths.

Instantly I huddled back down into the boat and then cautiously peered over the side. The figure burst to the surface and splashing water caught the sunlight. I squinted into the glare and watched the swimmer's steady, graceful progress towards the dock. He placed his hands firmly on it and hoisted himself up with one sure motion. His body gleamed in the sunshine and my eyes traveled down the broad tanned back to his lean flanks, his slender, straight legs.

"Shut up, Shiloh," he called. "You want the whole damned bunch of them down here?" The dog ran up to him. He patted its head affectionately, picked up a towel, and began to dry his hair. And then he turned towards the center of the lake. Facing me.

I had never seen a naked man. A mat of dark, thick hair on his chest narrowed to a seam down his flat stomach and gathered again, as if protectively, around a smooth, relaxed tube of flesh. His hips were slender, supporting his torso and firm, upraised arms. Even at this distance I could see a long, white scar zigzagging across his right thigh. He seemed vulnerable, graceful, and incredibly beautiful until I remembered that Eugene Duckworth was also a man. James Favour was also a man. I dove back to the bottom of the boat.

"Good boy, Shiloh. What is it? You want to play? Let me get my clothes on." The dog continued to bark excitedly. "What's the matter with you?" His voice carried effortlessly over the water. "See a squirrel out there, do you? You've seen squirrels before."

The voice, if not the tone, was oddly familiar. I looked

over the edge of the *Francesca*. I confess I watched him slide into his pants and pull his shirt over his tanned shoulders before I so much as looked at his bearded face, and then I realized I was looking at young Dr. Hamilton, not quite in the flesh anymore. He walked towards the boathouse, found a stick, threw it into the woods for Shiloh, and then returned to the dock, shading his eyes against the sun. "Who's out there? Is anyone there?"

I curled tighter in the bottom of the boat, but my movement only served to make the *Francesca* rock.

"Who's out in that boat?" he demanded. "Come out before I come get you. You'll wish I didn't," he added vehemently.

There was nothing else to do but sit up. Certainly there was nothing to say. What could I have answered? It's just the Ugly Duckling out here, waiting to become a swan?

I rowed with my back towards him, slowly moving to the dock. I realized, glancing down at my dirty nightdress with its bedraggled ribbons and shredded hem, that underneath I was naked, as he had been only moments before. Well, there was no help for it. I comforted myself with the only useful thing I ever learned at Merrywell College: if you cannot redeem the circumstances, ignore them.

I did not look over my shoulder at him, not once, not till I heard his inflectionless voice say "Hand me the line and I'll tie it up." I did as he asked. He gave me his hand and I scrambled from the boat. He dropped my hand and we stared at each other in a mutually hostile silence.

"Are you in the habit of watching nude men?" he demanded.

"Are you in the habit of trespassing?" I retorted in an imperious tone I realized I had borrowed from Charlotte.

"You don't look well, Miss Beale."

"Is that your professional opinion or an esthetic judgment?"

"An observation. I don't imagine anyone who spent the

night cramped up in a boat would look well. What were you doing out there?"

"I might ask you the same question," I answered, though the memory of last night stole over me and involuntarily I shuddered despite the morning sun.

"Allow me, Miss Beale, you look cold." He unbuttoned his shirt and took it off and handed it to me. "I don't imagine the sight of my chest will offend you after what you've just seen."

"I didn't mean to look. I wasn't spying, I just woke up and—there you were."

"There *you* were. What were you doing in that boat?"

"Nothing." I buttoned the shirt hurriedly. "And anyway, how do you know my name? I don't recall that Charlotte introduced us."

"No, your aunt has singularly bad manners, doesn't she? I know your name because I know all about Belle Haven. One must know one's enemies before he can defeat them."

"Do you intend to defeat me, Dr. Hamilton?"

The expression in his eyes softened at the same moment that his voice hardened. "I intend to get what I want from your aunt." Even Dr. Hamilton had begun to sound like Charlotte; perhaps she had infected us both. "You better sit down. You don't look altogether steady."

"I'm fine."

But he took me by the shoulders and led me to the edge of the dock. We sat with the sun at our backs, our shadows rippling and merging on the water. When I looked at him I realized his eyes were the same amber-green as the lake itself.

"You surprised me, Miss Beale. I didn't think anyone ever came to this lake anymore. Certainly not at dawn."

"You come here often?"

"Almost every day. Dawn is the only time I have that's not spoken for. Shiloh needs the run and I need the ride. It clears my head."

"To come to Belle Haven? I thought you hated Belle Haven."

"Don't mistake my presence here," he said tersely.

"For what? It seems to me that Belle Haven is the last place you'd ride to—at dawn or any other time."

He seemed to shrug. "I guess I come from force of habit. It's a ride I know well. I used to come here often as a boy. I hid out in those trees over there." He pointed across the lake, where green light and watery reflections twinkled intermittently. "Only then I didn't come at dawn. Then, I came to have a look at my father. My mother never knew," he added.

"And did you see him?"

"They used to have lots of bathing parties at this lake and I hid in the trees and watched my father. Once he and Charlotte were out in a boat alone. Father was rowing and Charlotte tended the champagne and then I saw him stop, as if he knew I was there, watching him."

"What did you do?"

"What was there to do?"

"Nothing, I guess."

He swung his feet over the water. "It is odd, my coming here, much as I hate Belle Haven, but it's the only place I could ever feel close to my father. I could never admire him, or even like him, but I always feel like I have a right to this lake. To be here."

"Because you love him?"

"I don't love him. I never actually exchanged words with him after he left my mother. I never saw him again, except from those woods, watching this lake."

"But you lived in Oakstone."

"It wasn't a matter of distance. It was a matter of pride. Or, perhaps I overestimate my importance to him. Perhaps he never really cared anyway."

"I'm sure he did."

"Why?"

"He was your father, wasn't he? He would have to care."

"Fatherhood's a biological phenomenon. There's nothing that says it must touch a man's heart."

Having had so little experience with my own father, I had nothing to offer. "But you kept coming to the lake?"

"No. I went away to school. Oakstone is a small town and even when I was very young I knew that people looked at me—looked at us, my mother and me—with a sort of curious pity that was intolerable. My mother knew it too. She stayed here, but I went to school where I could have a life untainted by scandal. My father paid for it. At least he paid the school bills."

"You sound as if you still despise him."

"Oh I do," he replied rather too hurriedly.

"But you became a doctor just like him."

"Not just like him."

A fresh wind came up off the lake and I could tell the brutal week of heat had been broken and the day would be fine and clear. We sat side by side and a curious camaraderie seemed to have sprung up between us, as though sharing an affection for the lake united us as friends, in spite of everything else. He told me about his time at the university (on scholarships) and that he never would have become a doctor at all, except for the War.

"You were in the War?"

"Only briefly. But long enough to learn a respect for human suffering, to have some pity for these poor frail carcasses of ours, to want to prolong life—my own and others'."

"Is that where you got the scar?" I asked and then I blushed furiously, but he seemed to laugh.

"On my right thigh? That scar?"

"Please don't embarrass me, Dr. Hamilton."

"Anyone who knows I have a scar on my right thigh ought at least to call me Bay."

"I thought your name was William."

"William Bayard Hamilton the Third, but I dropped the William when I was still a child. When my father ran off with your aunt, to be precise. I couldn't bear to carry the name."

I could not help but remember the shy and frightened child I had been, cursed with my father's name, which I could neither change nor deny—a name despised at Belle Haven. "It must have been terrible for you."

"Children are fragile creatures, Miss Beale."

"Please call me Dabney. I was orphaned very young too."

"Yes, but orphaned by death."

"You know about my parents?"

He turned to face me, seriously, as though weighing the merits of a flippant answer against the risks of a truthful one. "I told you, I know all about Belle Haven. I've made it my business to know."

"The enemy?"

"Yes, the enemy. Your parents died and that's a very different matter than being orphaned by desertion."

"Do you think so? Orphaned is orphaned. Alone is alone, no matter what the circumstances."

"Yes, but children see the world much more personally than adults do. Children believe themselves and everyone else to be accountable for what they do and so I thought that in some way I must be the one at fault, that I'd done something to drive my father from the house. I felt for a long time that it was my fault."

"When did you quit believing that?"

"When I discovered sex, Miss Beale. When that happened, I began at last to understand what drove my father, the power your aunt had over him."

I must have suddenly stiffened, because he very solicitously added, "I've shocked you; I'm sorry."

"Not at all. I'm nineteen, after all. I'm not shocked." Especially, I reflected grimly, when—after a fashion—I had discovered sex myself just the night before, cruel sex, wanton and vicious. I knew that much, though my limited imagination and lack of experience did not allow me to envision what it was Charlotte and Eugene had wanted from the hapless Favour. Still, I recognized their decadence and it made me nauseated all over again.

"You'll have to forgive me, Miss Beale."

"Dabney."

"Dabney. I'm not often in the company of young ladies and I sometimes forget the niceties they require."

I did not want to require niceties. Niceties would have somehow tainted the unambivalent honesty of our conversation. "So," I said with a careless toss of the head, "when did you discover sex?"

Bay laughed—a deep, easy, gentle laugh. He turned to me, his eyebrows lifted. "Do you really want to know?"

"Of course not," I replied. Not all my Merrywell training was lost on me.

Shiloh brought back his much-chewed stick and sniffed at me, evidently confused by the scent of Bay's shirt on a stranger. Bay patted the dog soothingly and finally Shiloh lay with his head on Bay's knee. "What were you doing out here in that boat all night?"

"I couldn't sleep," I said. It was after all the truth, or at least a part of it. I hastened to return the conversation to his own unexpected presence at the lake. "I'm very sorry about your father, Bay. No one ever told me he killed himself. I didn't know until the day you came to Belle Haven to see Charlotte."

"It was an ignoble end to an ignoble life," he said flatly.

"Did you hate him very much?"

"Not very much. I tried, but I couldn't really. But Belle Haven—I could hate that easily. Belle Haven and Charlotte

Fairchild and all that money and sex and power and the way the Fairchilds simply rode over people, as though it was all in sport. Like riding to hounds." Involuntarily I thought of the eyes of the fox in the dining-room mural. "I wanted to set up a practice far from here, bring my mother with me, but she insisted I return to Oakstone. I tried to argue with her, convince her we would be so much better off elsewhere, but she's one of those very frail, stubborn Virginia ladies. So I came back. I use my father's office, attached to the house."

"Maybe she thought you could come back and make up for what your father had done to—to your family's reputation."

"No. I thought of that, although it's possible. I only really understood her motives when she told me she wanted me to come to Belle Haven and get my father's things. That's what she had in mind all along and she knew it would take a long time and I would have to be here. She wants those documents and she could not do it for herself. Virginia ladies don't. But she couldn't do it now in any event, sick as she is. Anyway, I don't mind. It's the least I can do for her."

"What sort of documents are they?"

"We're not altogether sure. Certainly there was a suicide note. Beyond that"—he shrugged. "I'll get them for her, but I don't think they will be any comfort."

"Maybe, if she's dying, she doesn't care about comfort anymore. Maybe she just wants the truth."

Bay regarded me intently for a moment, with a gaze I might even have described as passionate, but then he got to his feet and said it was well past dawn and he had rounds to make. As he flung Shiloh's stick into the water his momentary truce with Belle Haven shattered. Suddenly I was part of Belle Haven again, no matter what I thought of it.

As we rose to walk to the boathouse, I winced and stumbled. Bay caught my arm. "Your feet!" He knelt instantly and touched my bruised and swollen feet.

"My shoes!" I froze, wondering where I had dropped them and how I could have run through the woods last night barefoot.

"I don't have my bag with me or I would tend to those feet. You'd better call Dr. Pruitt. They're badly scratched." He looked up at me. "You must have left the house in a hurry to have forgotten your shoes. Promise me you'll get those looked after."

"Yes. Of course."

He stood and said goodbye, walked toward his horse. I called after him. "Wait—your shirt!"

"Keep it."

"Oh no, I couldn't." I began to unbutton it hastily. If I were caught, I would have much more difficulty explaining a man's shirt than my torn and muddy nightgown. "Please, come take it back."

He walked towards me, holding his horse, the sunlight gleaming on the coppery hairs across his chest. I slid the shirt from my body and handed it to him. He put it on, but did not button it. Light sifted through the trees and fell over us— me in my soiled nightgown, his shirt hanging open from his shoulders. I did not raise my eyes to meet his. Indeed, I held my breath, believing that if I had moved a single muscle, he might have kissed me. Perhaps I flatter myself. But I know for certain if he had so much as swayed towards me, I certainly would have kissed him. As it was, though, he turned abruptly, mounted his horse, called his dog and rode away.

I started up the hill and I could hear his horse through the underbrush heading the other way. I knew that whatever else happened—indeed, if nothing else ever happened—I would always be grateful to Bay Hamilton, because at least I no longer felt tainted, irrevocably dirtied, by what I'd overheard the night before. He had unintentionally restored some equilibrium to my life, eased if not erased the fateful shocks of the night before. To this day I cherish the memory of Bay Hamilton swimming naked in the lake that morning, his body shining with sunlight and water, and of the scent of his shirt still clinging to my shoulders as I made my way back to Belle Haven.

6

Although my feet were sore and scratched, I ran quickly through the woods, to the small gate of the boxwood maze. I ducked down and scampered towards the house and the same laundry room I'd escaped from the night before. The grille was still open as I'd left it and, peering down, I could see the chair and the broken bottle of lye were exactly as I'd left them too.

I carefully lowered myself through the hole and landed feet first on the chair, which teetered dangerously but did not fall over. Sidestepping the pool of lye I jumped to the floor. I thought I would close the grilled window later, from the outside.

Carefully I opened the laundry-room door. The basement passage was empty, though I could hear Ethel the cook singing in the kitchen and the scullery maid banging pots in the sink. Quickly and silently I made my way to the servants' stairwell. As I passed the butler's pantry, I caught a glimpse of Favour's shining head bent over some silver. He did not look up.

I was in fact spared the sight of Favour's blue eyes and Charlotte's cruel face until dinnertime that evening. Only

Austin, Charlotte, and I were present. Eugene, Charlotte informed me, had gone back to Oakstone in the morning, for which I was grateful: nothing ever escaped Eugene, but Charlotte and Austin were too self-absorbed to notice that I—simple Dabney—was a fundamentally changed woman, that I had lost my innocence, by accident perhaps, but lost it all the same.

Staring at Charlotte over the candles and the cold white roses in the center of the table, I searched her face for some trace of depravity, but found nothing. Her skin was flawless, untainted as the smooth pearls around her neck. I thought surely such degeneracy must have left—

"What are you staring at, Dabney?"

"Nothing."

"I wish you'd learn some manners."

"I'm sorry, Charlotte."

"Favour! Come pour Dabney some water. She needs it. She needs something," Charlotte muttered under her breath.

Favour poured me the water and I thanked him. Favour too seemed absolutely unchanged. Not so much as a ripple of suffering disfigured his even features, not a crease or pinch or pucker, and his blue eyes were so empty as to appear sightless. Throughout dinner Charlotte referred to him in the cold oblivious tone she always used with servants and he responded like a well-bred dog, not the whimpering cur he'd been the night before.

I could not eat; everything tasted acrid and metallic. I gazed at the mural my father had painted and the sight of the dogs tearing at the fox's flesh only further sickened and depressed me. Caesar seemed to sense my revulsion and kept one blood-shot eye on me, as if he were Eugene's understudy.

In his usual way Austin finished his dinner in ravenous gulps. He had probably been dry, maybe even sober all after-noon, since his very jowls trembled and his skin was white and waxy. He motioned to Favour to pour him some more wine, downed that, and then another few glasses, and then fastened his bleary but not unkind gaze on me. "If you don't eat your dinner, Dabney, you can't have dessert."

"I don't want dessert."

"It is the Lord's bounty, given to the chosen and thee would do well not to spurn it."

"Thee would do well!" Charlotte crowed. "Lord, Austin, will your affectations never cease?"

Austin spluttered, "I follow the ways of the Book and the speech of the Saviour, holy speech, not profane like thine, Charlotte."

"Do the ways of the Book encourage you to drink yourself into a blithering stupor, night and day?"

"The Lord loves even the lowliest of his flock." Austin bent his balding head over his plate.

"Yes, well, the lowliest of his flock costs me a bloody fortune. Prohibition is more expensive than sin," Charlotte quipped and with that she left us, a long peach-colored scarf and the odor of Rappaccini cologne trailing behind her.

I excused myself to Austin, who seemed not to have heard me, so as I passed by him, I touched his shoulder and he patted my hand and returned to his wine.

I followed Charlotte into the library, where she was fanning herself with a half-open book. "Ring for Favour, will you, Dabney? If I don't have a gin I'll melt in this murderous heat."

I did as she asked and waited till she ordered and Favour had left before I began. "I'd like a word with you please, Charlotte," I said more timidly than I intended.

"Can't it wait, Dabney? I can tell from the sound of your squeaky little voice it's going to be tiresome."

"No, it can't wait."

Favour returned with the gin bottle, a tall glass, and an ice bucket. I concentrated on the picture above Charlotte's head, a portrait of the four little Fairchild girls, all wearing blue dresses and white stockings and clutching the relics of childhood. Caesar, still watchful, followed Favour in and found a cool corner.

"Will that be all, madame?"

"For the time being, yes."

At this exchange, my very skin crawled. Charlotte lifted two glittering ice cubes into her glass with silver tongs; she poured the gin in a silvery cascade. "Well, what is it? Don't sit there like Marian. Out with it. I don't have all night."

I'm sure you don't, I thought, but I began more tentatively. "It's about money, Charlotte; well, it is and it isn't."

"Whatever is not about money always turns out to be about money after all, so you might as well be frank about it."

"I've been thinking, Charlotte, it's July now and Alicia isn't due back for months and I don't want to go to college anymore and you probably don't want to have me hanging around here."

"Really, Dabney, 'hanging around' makes you sound like laundry."

I felt like laundry at the moment, wet, limp, and soiled. "I want to leave Belle Haven, Charlotte."

"Really?" Her eyes flickered with interest and she carried her glass back with her to a reclining position. "Aren't you happy here, Dabney dear? Have we been nasty and neglectful?"

"I'm serious, Charlotte."

"That's your trouble, Dabney, you're always serious. So bloody serious. Just like your father."

"I don't see what he has to do with it."

"Get on with it, Dabney. What's this got to do with money? You can leave on the next train for all I care."

"I'd like my part of the money now."

"What money?"

But I scarcely heard her, indeed I scarcely heard myself. My words tumbled from my lips, heedless as water tripping over stones. I heard myself promising to sign any sort of document Eugene drew up, I promised to go and never return, never to claim another thing from Charlotte or Belle Haven. I cajoled and promised and nattered obsessively until Charlotte rose from the couch, walked to the ice bucket, and studied me as she poured another gin. "What money?" she repeated.

"My share of Grandfather's money. I mean, my mother's share. I know you're holding it in trust till I'm twenty-one, but I'm nineteen now and if you'll just let me have it now, I'll—"

"What money?"

"Francesca told me. She told me about the trust fund, but you mustn't be angry with her. She told me not to tell and I wouldn't have except that I really want to leave Belle Haven and I hate to spoil your surprise, Francesca told me it was to be a surprise—"

"And I'm sure it will. What else did Francesca tell you?"

"The money—that Grandfather divided his money up equally among all his daughters and you're holding mine till I'm twenty-one. You're my guardian," I added pointlessly.

"Francesca is a dolt. A lovely, gullible, enchanting dolt." Charlotte plucked an ice cube from her glass and ran it luxuriously around her face and then tossed it in a nearby potted palm. "Let me set you straight, Dabney, because it's clear that poor dear Francesca has badly misguided you. You shouldn't trust Francesca when it comes to money. You know she hasn't got the slightest bit of sense regarding money."

I did know this, but I said nothing.

"Your grandfather—my dear Daddy—did divide up his money among us four, but that was before your mother ran off to England with a second-rate dabbler."

"He wasn't second rate."

"He was."

"You let him paint your portrait, didn't you?"

Charlotte took a steep, harsh breath, as though the wind had been momentarily knocked out of her. "Don't be insolent. It can scarcely have escaped even your benighted notice that your grandfather bore you no great love. Daddy had his faults, I admit, and one of them was that he carried grudges. He carried them everywhere he went. Daddy never forgot a thing." She snipped each word off her lips as if with pinking shears and her eyes gleamed with what I sensed even then was enjoyment. "And when I say he never forgot, I should add that he never forgave either. He was like that. He changed his will so that only Francesca and Alicia and I would inherit anything."

"I don't believe you."

"Ask Eugene. Eugene was Daddy's lawyer."

"But Francesca—"

"Oh, damn Francesca. She never listens to anything that doesn't involve her personally and immediately. Who knows what Francesca thought she heard? Daddy always said that Alicia and I got all the brains in the family. Francesca and Julia were hopeless. Francesca still is, but at least she had better sense than Julia. At least she didn't run off with a man who was little better than a servant, an unfaithful servant at that."

"My father was never a servant," I said stoutly. "He was a great artist."

Charlotte's laughter jangled like broken glass. She tossed her head and stared at me from beneath her effective stray curl. "Poor Julia, no brains, no taste, and certainly no sense. I hate to disillusion you, my dear, but your father was allowed to stay on at Belle Haven like any servant—which is to say, only as long as he did his job and did it well. Only in his case, there was some question about what his job was.

He thought it was to make poor Julia fall in love with him and marry him—yes, marry a grubby second-rate painter so that he could get his grubby second-rate hands on her fortune."

"That's not so!"

"Oh yes, it is. Daddy gave Anthony Beale everything he could ever have wanted, a place to work, a place to live, paints, canvas, commissions, not just for the paintings at Belle Haven, oh no, from all over the county and beyond. When people knew there was an artist in residence at Belle Haven, they knew he was good, because Daddy cultivated only the best."

"You see, I told you he wasn't second rate."

Charlotte seemed momentarily confused. "Even Daddy's judgment was known to fail. But be that as it may—Anthony Beale had everything a man could wish for at Belle Haven, but that wasn't enough. He was greedy. Just like you are greedy. He wanted nothing less than one quarter of the Fairchild money and that, my dear greedy little niece, is why he seduced your mother, yes, humped her in the fields like a dog for all I know, got her stuffed up with you, probably thinking that Daddy would be so happy not to have a bastard brat on his hands that he'd bless their marriage with lots of money and that he wouldn't care that his daughter had laid down and spread herself to a man with paint-stained hands who always smelled of turpentine. Well, Daddy wasn't like that. Anthony Beale wired here after they'd got some drunken justice of the peace out of bed one night to marry them in his suspenders, Anthony Beale wired and expected to be welcomed home like the prodigal son-in-law. But he hadn't counted on Daddy. No indeed. Daddy wired him back. He dictated the message to me, so I know exactly what Daddy thought. He wired: *Be damned to you both.*"

Charlotte opened a mother-of-pearl inlay box and took out

a cigarette. The match made a bone-chilling hiss, and as she turned to me her face was obscured in a cloud of smoke. "You look very sick, Dabney. Shall I ring for Favour? No? Well then, let's just have it out, shall we?" She took a deep drag. "I tried to warn Julia. I told her that's what Daddy would do, but she wouldn't listen. Julia was absolutely under Anthony's spell. Sick with love. Positively putrid with love. It was disgusting. I told Anthony too. I told him he'd never get a penny of her money, but he didn't believe me. He never believed me."

Charlotte smashed out her cigarette and threw the butt into the cold fireplace, and as she walked toward me I could feel the hairs at the back of my neck prick and curl, but not with fear, something else.

"I even tried to help them. I tried to convince Daddy not to disinherit Julia altogether. I told him—blame me if you must."

"You?"

"I brought Anthony Beale to Belle Haven. What did you think? That he magically appeared at the servants' entrance one day with his hand out? I spent the 1898 season in London. He painted my portrait there. I felt sorry for him. I was the one who suggested to Daddy that he might be a good painter for Belle Haven. What a fool I was. What a blind little fool," she added vehemently. But vehemence was never Charlotte's style; she collected herself quickly with a brittle laugh. "Your mother told you he died before you came to New York, didn't she?"

"Yes," I said miserably.

"Well, she lied to you, Dabney dear. He didn't die. When Anthony Beale found out Julia'd been disinherited, he left her. And you. That shocks you, doesn't it? Well, you need some shocks. Julia needed some shocks too and she got them, poor thing. I went to New York and I told her I was certain I could talk Daddy into letting her come back to Belle Haven, but dear little Julia said she had her pride. Well, that's damned well all she had and more's the pity for you, Dabney."

She came towards me and took my chin in her long-fingered hands and yanked it up so I had no choice but to look into her gold-gleaming eyes. "Julia might have had her pride, but you've got nothing, not a nickel in the world except what I choose to give you. And don't you forget it." She released me and waltzed back to her chair. "I've even paid for your education, apparently fruitlessly, since all you seem to have learned is that cows won't go down stairs."

"I don't believe it."

"You proved it. Cows won't go down stairs."

"I don't believe anything you've said. My father died in 1904, run over by a hansom cab in London on his way home."

"Oh Lordy, is that what she told you? Oh, Julia was desperate, wasn't she? Your father didn't die until—let me think, 1916, I think it was, a mere five years ago. He didn't give a damn about you, my dear. He left your mother and didn't give a damn about you and blew his brains out, so I heard, in 1916. Please, Dabney, don't faint on the library carpet. At least have the grace to go to your room to faint and weep."

"I'm not going to faint." But I was; the blood drained from my head and seemed to collect in the pit of my stomach and I had to sit down.

"I don't know why it should surprise you. It didn't surprise me. It didn't surprise me when he deserted his wife and child and it didn't surprise me when he committed suicide. Pretentious people often commit suicide, people who think they're very talented and destined for greatness. They kill themselves when they realize that they're second rate and all the world knows it. That's when they do all that unpleasant brain-blowing and wrist-slitting. Messy."

An ignoble end to an ignoble life. Bay's voice echoed in my ears.

"... That's why I never worry about Austin, hopeless drunk that he is. Austin never had any pretensions, never believed himself destined for something special. That's why he'll go on living. He'll probably outlive me. What do you think, Dabney?" Her lips curled around the question. "Will Austin outlive me?"

I stared at the flowers worked into the Persian carpet. I believed her, but I could not dwell on that now. Now I had to extract myself from this with some shred of dignity and it was as if Bay came to my rescue. I chose my words with a jeweler's precision. "I'm sure you know all about suicides, Charlotte. You were married to one. Why didn't your daddy disinherit you? You were slut enough to run off with a married man."

I got no further. Charlotte was out of her chair as if she'd been hurled from the mouth of a cannon. She shot across the room and slapped me so hard my ears rang, my very brains rattled in my skull.

"If you ever mention that again, I'll, I'll—" Her chest and shoulders were heaving, her lips twisted, and then she spoke more calmly, but through her teeth. "Don't forget, Dabney, you haven't an ounce of talent, an iota of brains, or a grain of beauty. All you have is me."

I commanded my body to move, and to my everlasting surprise it did—bone and brain and muscle working in conscious unison got me out of the library and into the hall. On my way towards the stairs, I paused at the dining-room door and stared at Anthony Beale's mural painted across the wall: beautiful Belle Haven, a white diadem set in the distance, with Charles Fairchild, booted, spurred, and mounted, leading his four lovely daughters in the hunt—the rich, the wellborn, riding towards a destiny dictated by a bunch of slavering dogs. And when I looked again at that fox—the bloody, half-gnawed, still-living fox—I saw that its eyes were unmistakably Charlotte Courtney's eyes: narrowed, glinting gold, and filled—just as they had been moments ago in the library—with triumph and malice.

The eyes of that fox, the sound of Charlotte's hard, ringing, crystal laugh haunted my dreams, and I spent the next week in parched delirium. All I remember with any certainty was Marian's light footfall, her cool hand across my burning forehead, and water dripping into a basin as she wrung out cloths to bathe my face. The water drops echoed and ferried my inflamed imagination back to Bay Hamilton's lean, glistening body gliding through the lake. I heard, or thought I heard, someone say they would call the doctor and I smiled and slept fitfully, reaching in my dream for Bay's outstretched hand.

But when I woke I stared into the watery red-rimmed eyes of Dr. Pruitt, a man as pale and thin and insubstantial as a chalk drawing, and so I drifted back to the naked doctor of my reveries.

Austin was very good to me during my convalescence. He brought his faithful bottle and *David Copperfield* into my room and read to me in his quaking voice for hours at a time. I appreciated the effort, but I remember little of *David Copperfield*. My thoughts were elsewhere. I walked back through the forest of lies and truth, through what Charlotte had told me, what my mother had told me, what little I could remember on my own. A growing bitterness lodged in my heart, my very soul. I did not begrudge my mother her lies. But my father. How could he? How could he have abandoned her? How could he have lived till 1916 and never so much as asked after me? What was it Bay had said? Fatherhood was a biological condition and there's nothing that says it must touch a man's heart. But surely my father . . . my own father. I began to hate my mother, too, for having protected his memory, for harboring love for a man who had been so cruel to us both. And suicide. Was there no end to the ugliness? I so much better understood Bay's attitude towards his father. And then I wondered—if Charlotte was right and only the pretentious commit suicide, what sort of pretensions had the elder Dr. Hamilton cherished? What dashed dreams drove him to turn the scalpel on himself? Ignoble ends for ignoble lives. Ignoble men and faithless fathers.

Charlotte, although she never stayed to read or chat, called on me at least once a day while I was recovering. She acted as if nothing had happened. Quite the contrary. She lavished her charm upon me as if it were a scented veil. She brought in bright armloads of golden day lilies and arranged them in my room, chatting amiably about her daily rides on Dancer, about Caesar's antics, Eugene's doings (Eugene never came to see me), her new hairdresser. She brought letters and postcards from Francesca and Alicia. In short, she performed and I applauded. There never was a declared truce between us, because Charlotte refused to acknowledge the slightest shred of war.

But Charlotte's charm was rather like those fragile lilies: once she left, the illusions she cultivated left with her and I spent long hours worrying about the past, which I could not

change, and dreading the future, before which I was pow-
erless. Charlotte was right about me. I was a freckled, long-
legged, undistinguished weed in the Fairchild garden of
beauties. I hadn't a shred of talent or skills or education that
might have fit me for useful work (save, perhaps, for teaching,
which I dreaded) and I knew that unlike the plucky heroines
of the novels I'd read, there was small chance I could make
my own way in the world. The future loomed before me—
an ominous void. My resolve to leave Belle Haven wilted in
the face of all these undeniable truths—these and one other.
I knew I could not leave Belle Haven without seeing Bay
Hamilton at least once more. To tell him that I understood
his rage against Belle Haven and all it stood for. To tell him
that I shared it. To tell him that I had not been orphaned by
death, but rather by desertion. To tell him nothing at all. To
see him.

I buried my face in my pillow and might have burst into
tears again, but I felt a tap on my shoulders and whirled
around to see Marian staring at me. In her hands she held
the shoes I'd lost the night I bolted down the laundry chute
a thousand years ago. Marian's eyes were full of curiosity.
She took a small scrap of paper and a pencil from her apron
pocket and scribbled, "Laundry bin."

"I can't imagine how they got there."

Marian put her fingers to my lips and smiled. She took the
shoes and placed them in the closet and left the room as
silently as she'd come.

I recovered long before Austin finished with *David Copperfield,* though he was kind enough to leave it by my bed.
He might have laughed if he'd known that I would not complete the book until I was seventy-five. Literature offers little
for the young; life is too pressing.

As soon as I was well enough, one morning in early August,
I woke at dawn, dressed quickly, and opened my door, hoping

not to meet anyone as I tore down the staircase and out of the house. I so longed to see Bay that, when I got to the lake, I imagined him everywhere, his voice rustling through the fully leafed trees, his form splashing through the collage of light and shadow on the water, but I was quite alone. I went the next day and the day after that and the day following, when, as my feet crashed through the dawn-lit woods, I could hear Shiloh barking. When I arrived at the lake I saw Bay standing on the dock.

We ran towards each other and stopped. Bay offered me his hand and I gave him mine like the lady I was trained to be. "I've looked for you," he said. "I wondered if— I thought maybe—"

"I've been ill."

"You look it. Your eyes, I mean."

He released my hand and we walked side by side, our shoulders touching, towards the boathouse. Bay went in and emerged carrying oars for the *Alicia*. I waited outside, because I felt if I had followed him in, I might have ignited that decrepit boathouse, so intense was the flint and tinder of our meeting. We stepped in the boat and rowed out to the middle of the lake and into each other's lives. I remember little of our conversation, only that it was charged with longing. I must have told him some of my conversation with Charlotte and what she'd told me of my father's death and how I too was the child of a suicide.

"Do you hate her very much?" he asked.

"Hate Charlotte?" Actually I was rather stunned by the notion of hating Charlotte. It had never occurred to me. I despised her of course after what I knew of her sexual proclivities, but I did not mention those and said only that I didn't hate her as much as I now detested my father for what he'd done to my mother and me.

Bay rested lightly on the oars and I dipped my fingers into

the lake. Overhead birds scattered across the sky and pep-
pered the surrounding trees. Finally Bay said, "I hate Charlotte Courtney. I wish I didn't, but I do. Duckworth's no
better. I've been to see him several times. I've been to another
lawyer too, who tells me that they've every right to hold on
to my father's things. I'll never get hold of my father's things
unless they choose to give them to me."

"Have you told your mother that?"

"My mother looks at me gently and says 'Keep trying, keep
trying.' "

"What will you do?"

"I don't know. There's a county judge, Judge Vail, who's
well respected and a fair man, and I thought I might appeal
to him. Maybe if the request came from someone other than
me . . . maybe if Charlotte feared the old scandal would be
raked up, she might—"

"But raking up the scandal—wouldn't that hurt your
mother?"

"Nothing can hurt her now. She's too close to death."

I reached out impulsively and put my hand over his in
what I thought was a gesture of sympathy, but he recognized
my desire and pulled me towards him. He drew me into
his arms and brought my face to his and kissed me. I held
him as his lips traveled over my face and hair. "Dabney,
Dabney—I shouldn't—it's not right—" I put my hands over
his mouth, and his lips moved against my palm and his hazel
eyes swept over my face. "I was so afraid I'd never see you
again. I kept coming back to the lake, always against my better
judgment."

"Oh Bay—I would have been here, I would have been
back the very next day, but I got sick. Oh, I've wanted you
too. I've thought of nothing but you."

He kissed me again and again and I felt for his kisses what
Austin Courtney must have felt for alcohol—they were ad-
dictive, seductive, and if I could have made a bargain at that

moment with the gods or the devil—it little mattered which—
I would have promised my very soul to remain rocking forever in that small boat, my body between Bay's knees, my
lips pressed to his, my fingers exploring his face, and his hands
traveling over my body. I thought for a moment that surely
the boat must have capsized, because I was drowning in a
pool of sensation.

Whatever conversation passed between us after that was
punctuated with kisses. We laughed to hear ourselves and
nearly wept when we had to part. Bay had early morning
calls, but he swore he would be back the following morning
and I said yes, yes, I'd be there too, tomorrow and the day
after and the day after that—that I would be at that lake
forever.

And in some ways, I was true to my word, because in the
following weeks the diurnal course of time seemed to cease;
day after summer day the dawns merged into one another
the way that eddies in the wake of the *Alicia* flowed effortlessly, seamlessly into fluid patterns.

Each morning I returned to Belle Haven (after carefully
scraping the telltale mud from my shoes) refreshed, restored,
imbued with a happiness and confidence that did not escape
Eugene's critical eyes.

"You seem awfully lively these days, Dabney," he said to
me one morning, "very lively indeed for so early in the morning. Have you taken up some worthy pastime—like bird-
watching or nature walks perhaps?"

His voice was so coarse and insinuating that at first I
thought only to deflect his question or mumble something
inane, but instead I snapped back, "None of your damn business, Eugene." I was not the Ugly Duckling anymore and
never would be again.

"My, my, I was only inquiring, Dabney, no need to be
snippy. It's just you seem more the butterfly these days than
your usual caterpillar self."

"Don't pry into my life, Eugene, and I won't pry into yours."

I wanted to say something more, to make him worry about what I knew about his own secrets, but I held my tongue. Indeed, I never even betrayed them to Bay, if betray is the word. For one thing, I don't believe I could have begun to describe what I overheard and for another, I always tried to avoid discussing Charlotte and Belle Haven. I always knew that they stood between me and Bay in some unalterable and as yet unfathomed way, but I did not wish to be reminded of that fact nor did I wish Bay to be reminded. We were young, after all, and on those pearlescent dawns we steered clear of the shoals of the past, but I knew even then that the future was equally treacherous.

But for the moment we had the present. We sat on the diving board, my head in Bay's lap, Bay stroking my neck and back, talking as the sun rose up over the trees and Bay's bare toes rippled the water. We rowed out to the middle of the lake in the *Alicia* or the *Francesca* (never, never the *Charlotte*), we took walks in the woods surrounding the lake. And of course there eventually came that morning when words failed us, as they eventually fail all lovers, and we spoke with our bodies.

I lay on my back in the boathouse, staring up at the blasted roof and the still dewy sky, and Bay's fingers trembled over the buttons on my blouse and his hand slipped up my skirt. I tingled in every pore, every nerve and hair, the very marrow of my bones electrified with desire as Bay Hamilton ran his hands over my body.

But Bay balked at the final act, that day and the following days. Each morning I rose at dawn and went down to the lake fully expecting to become Bay's lover in the fullest sense of the word; I offered him my virginity, but he demurred and I found myself returning to the house moist, spongy with desire, and aware—vitally aware—of a throbbing that I never guessed possible. It was as if my body and I parted company and the body remained expectant, famished, while I grew increasingly irritable, even angry, unknowing and (probably because of my last morsel of virginal reticence) unwilling to ask Bay the obvious. Why?

One morning as I was getting dressed in the first gray light of dawn, I simply neglected to put on any underclothes at all. I threw on a loose shift and took a heavy sweater so I could cover myself if I met anyone when coming back. Thus lightly clad I flew to the boathouse and was naked when Bay arrived. I slid my arms around his neck and pressed myself against him so that his buttons bit into my flesh. "I want you to love me, Bay. You've loved other women—why not me?"

He murmured against my hair as he stroked my back in undulating currents, "I've had other women. I've loved only you. More than you'll ever know. More than I can tell you."

"Then don't tell me." I drew him down, unbuttoned his shirt and pants. "I want you. All of you."

"There's a risk," he said hoarsely, "a terrible risk."

"I don't care. Nothing matters but you and me."

"That's not true."

"It is. I don't care if I get pregnant. I'd welcome it. I love you so much I can't bear not having you and I don't care."

"But I do, Dabney. You don't understand. We can never be ordinary lovers who fall in love and get married and have children."

"Why not?"

"Not us, Dabney. If we took our love from this lake, from this little place, it would perish like an orchid in the snow."

"That's not so. I'll love you till the day I die."

"It would perish nonetheless." He broke away from me gently and his eyes lit with pain and confusion. "Because you have a vengeful aunt and I have a dying mother."

"She can't live forever." I was ashamed of that, but continued unrepentantly, "You're all that matters to me. Love me, Bay."

"I do love you."

"Really love me." I drew him down again. "Really love me," I whispered fiercely.

"What if you got pregnant?"

"I told you, I don't care. I love you."

"And I love you. Do you think I could ever perform an abortion on you?"

"Abortion?" I was stung by the irrevocable grimness of the word. It was the sort of word that lurks just outside the pristine confines of Merrywell College. "It's illegal."

"That doesn't stop its being done."

"But I'm—we're different."

"No, we're not. That's one thing being a doctor teaches you. Everyone is exactly the same, Dabney, they only think they're different till they get caught being exactly the same. I could never perform that operation on you."

"You wouldn't have to," I pleaded.

"Take my word for it," he said tersely, "we have this time and this place together and that's all we have. When that's gone—"

"Gone?" Suddenly my skin prickled and I shivered.

"There are things you don't understand, forces outside of us—"

"Don't talk to me like that." I sat up and shook free of him. "Forces I don't understand—what do you think I am? A child?"

"I only meant—"

"I know what you meant. I'm not a simpleton after all. You meant that you've been lying all along and suddenly I'm about to become demanding and inconvenient and now you want to ride out of here feeling virtuous that you've left me my virginity. Taken my love and left my virginity."

"This can only get worse with words." He stood and began to button his clothes.

"The great Dr. Hamilton. So thoughtful. Thank you for my virginity. Thank you for being so kind." I was at a disadvantage, being naked, but I refused to cower and cover myself.

"You don't understand."

"I understand everything. You've come here all these weeks and sullied yourself with a bit of Belle Haven, had your revenge, and now you're done with it and with me. You've revenged yourself on Charlotte Courtney with my body and my love."

"Are you mad, Dabney?"

"Mad, angry, yes—"

"How can you say these things? I love you."

"No, you've had me—oh wait, I almost forgot I'm still a virgin. Should I be grateful? Should I think you noble?"

"I'm not noble."

"You're certainly not, you lying dog. You've revenged yourself on me and I hate the sight of you."

"Dabney, don't let us part this way." He knelt down and took my bare shoulders in his hands. "God, how I want you, Dabney, but we haven't got any future, we—"

"Liar. Maybe you're not a liar, maybe you're just what Charlotte said you were—a sanctimonious prig."

He didn't reply. He simply left me and walked out. His horse whinnied and Shiloh barked in exuberant greeting and I listened to him ride away till finally the very sound of the hooves died. Naked I walked outside and realized that for months I had not seen the world as it really was. For months, always the vision of Bay's face had wavered between me and whatever world there was. For months I had lived only for the dawn-lit hours we'd had together, for Bay's voice and hands and lips and lingering presence. Now I noticed that

the world had changed. The windswept trees, the protective
hills were still green, though not the ebullient green of summer but a dimmed and dusty green. A few desultory leaves
spun over my head and skimmed the waters of the lake and
autumn was upon us.

Part II

8

Autumn at Belle Haven brought the return of the hunting season and its attendant festivities. The Belle Haven Hunt Ball had been held the second Saturday in October for as long as anyone could remember and neither death nor war had ever intervened. Even Austin was allowed to participate in this gala and he knew better than to misbehave.

Past autumns I'd been at school, but this year Charlotte insisted I not only attend the ball, but that I ride in the hunt as well. I reminded her I was not fond of horses and was a mediocre rider at best. She retorted that I was a very bad rider indeed, but insisted nonetheless that an Oakstone tailor come out and fit me for a riding habit. The tailor could have measured me for a shroud and I would not have cared, so paralyzed was I with misery in those weeks. The lake was closed to me. I could not bear to return there. I spent my days mute and miserable and my nights tossing sleeplessly. I had cultivated passions I could neither relieve nor deny and I was obsessed with my lover's perfidy.

Eugene was quick to notice this new change in me. I played long hours on the piano while Charlotte was riding, and Eugene entered the salon one day and casually remarked that pianos were for playing, not attacking. I banged out a harsh chord and stalked away. "My, my," he said, "our little butterfly has become a caterpillar again, hasn't she?"

"I'm not well," I replied haughtily.

"Well, it's gone on too long for it to be your monthlies," he remarked with what I thought was unpardonable cheek, but he laughed at his own cleverness and left me disconsolate in the salon, staring at my mother's portrait.

Even Charlotte seemed to notice. "You look peaked, Dabney," she said one day at lunch as she tossed a chunk of raw meat to the ever-faithful Caesar. "I daresay the hunt will cheer you up."

"I hate horses and I'd rather not ride."

"Everyone at Belle Haven rides in the hunt. Everyone always has. Everyone always will."

"I'd rather stay behind and help with the preparations for the ball."

"That's why we have servants."

It was a crisp early October afternoon, the mums drying in the garden, the leaves beginning to turn and furl on the trees. Charlotte looked particularly beautiful, in a long burgundy sweater and a skirt of pale rose. She smiled coyly at Eugene. "Eugene can't ride either, but he makes a go of it, don't you, Eugene?"

"Have I any choice?"

"You simply have a few drinks first, Dabney. Ask Eugene. All the riders have a few drinks so their courage will be equal to their imagination."

"It wouldn't make any difference to me," I replied. "I don't trust horses and I don't like them. I think they're beautiful, but they're stupid and I don't want to entrust my bones to any stupid beast."

Favour brought the coffee pot and cups on a tray, and as he began to clear the dessert plates, Charlotte—for the first and last time—addressed him publicly with something less than a command. "What do you think, Favour?"

"Madame?"

"My niece says that horses are beautiful and stupid and not to be trusted."

"Madame?"

Charlotte poured the coffee without looking up. "I say that the reason God made them beautiful and stupid is so that they might be tamed by a superior intelligence." She handed Eugene his coffee. "If there's a riding accident, for instance, Favour, do you think it's the fault of a stupid rider or a stupid horse?" She handed me my coffee and I took it though my palms were slick with sweat: Charlotte was at her most dangerous when her voice had that teasing, toying ring. "A smart rider," she continued, "knows how to make a horse obey his every command. All the horse has to do is learn to obey. That's not such a hard lesson, is it, Favour? Not even for a stupid beast."

"No, madame." Then Favour spilled the tray of plates and some shattered. He knelt and picked up the pieces around Charlotte's feet. She ignored him, chatting with Eugene as Favour withdrew as inconspicuously as a clumsy man can.

For the hunt festivities, every rich county white person who could ride so much as a rocking horse would assemble at the Belle Haven stables early in the morning for the blessing of the hounds by the local pastor, and then we would all ride off after a pack of yammering dogs. After the hunt, we'd come back to Belle Haven for drinks and lunch, and then everyone would return to his respective home and reconvene at Belle Haven at eight, freshly powdered, coiffed, starched, and pressed, and ready for the ball that would probably last all night.

Ethel, the cook, convinced Charlotte to hire some extra servants. She cited an incident some years before when a

particularly drunken guest thought Marian was being impu-
dent for not saying "Yes, sir" when he addressed her. Ethel
also mentioned—as tactfully as possible—that Favour was
hopelessly inept and would only be more so at a large gathering. Charlotte agreed and Ethel selected the servants and
for a week Belle Haven rang with preparation and was
flooded with unfamiliar servile faces.

The day of the hunt I woke at dawn from a troubled and
inconstant sleep, haunted as always by the spectre of Bay and
the misery he'd given me, which had grown increasingly intolerable. Mine was a woman's unhappiness, I recognized
that. A child's sorrow can be assuaged, but a woman's is
boundless; it can be buried for the sake of endurance, concealed for the sake of appearance, but it can be assuaged only
by the same man who gave her that sorrow in the first place.
That morning I decided to perjure my pride and write Bay
a note of apology. The very next day, I resolved, I would
write to Bay and say whatever was necessary to bring him
back to my arms.

I took a bath and dressed in my new riding clothes. I tied
my hair with a black ribbon at my neck, but it refused to lie
sleekly and the ends still curled about my face. Still, I thought
as I surveyed the mirror, I cut a rather handsome figure. The
severe riding habit became me and I struck pose after pose,
as if I were going to paint my own portrait.

My self-satisfaction evaporated the minute I was seated on
my horse (Charlotte called her a nag), a beast named Dolly.
The men all seemed to be on high-stepping mounts called
Genghis and Attila, and the ladies sat astride (most of them,
though some still affected the old side saddle) beasts called
Cicero and Roanoke and Fancy. Not only her name, but the
nature of my horse set me apart from these people. Dolly
and I clung near the fence while everyone else trotted about,
exchanging greetings, talking, laughing, patting each other's
horses and each other's backs as the servants handed out

stirrup cups. Silver chalices were given to the riders, mere glasses handed out to the spectators who thronged the rim of the pasture enjoying the free illegal liquor while taking care to stay clear of the prancing hooves. We drank the sharp concoction of whiskey and lemon juice and sugar. "And prohibition be damned," I heard one beef-faced man exclaim as he pulled out a shiny silver flask from his boot and handed it round.

All—horses, men, women, even the servants and spectators—were groomed to perfection. I felt all the more clumsy and out of place; the ribbon in my hair was loose and my legs already ached; sensing my discomfort, Dolly was skittish and (so I thought) embarrassed.

"Do you think you'll still be on that horse when they catch the fox?" Eugene asked me.

"I hope they never catch the damn fox."

He rode off laughing and addressed his next remarks to the beef-faced man, whom I now recognized from the Fourth of July party. Their faces all meshed and though I recognized many of them from Charlotte's social set, I could not have called anyone by name. The men, in truth, all looked alike, with their well-fed faces and well-trained beasts. The women were a different matter: they sat stiffly, sure of themselves— young matrons, heavy-jowled grandmothers, and young girls—their backbones all girded against the slightest betrayal of fear, their chins and shoulders held at the correct angle, which they must have learned at schools like Merrywell. Had I ever known how to look that aloof?

Maintaining herself impeccably in the saddle, a young woman rode up beside me. She had a sharp face with bright blue eyes and the tiny rosebud mouth that was all the rage then. "Daphne, isn't it?" She smiled and reached out her hand in greeting. "I'm Marjorie Vail, Class of Nineteen."

I was afraid to let go of Dolly long enough to take her hand, and besides, Dolly seemed to have taken an instant dislike to her horse. I tried to rein her in as best I could.

"Class of Nineteen," she repeated gaily.

My expression must have resembled Favour's blank stare, because she frowned and then said, "Aren't you Charlotte's niece, Daphne?"

"Dabney."

"Yes, well, I'm Marjorie Vail. Class of Nineteen!"

"I'm sorry. I don't understand."

"Merrywell College. Don't you go to Merrywell? I distinctly thought someone said you went to Merrywell."

"I was expelled," I said before I realized I might have phrased it more gracefully than that.

The Master of the Hounds spared me further embarrassment by riding in with all the dogs in a pack. They broke and began sniffing the spectators and servants. The Master of the Hounds called them by name, though save for Caesar they all looked alike to me: muscular, salivating, shiny-toothed creatures.

Just then Charlotte chose to make her entrance. Clods flew from Dancer's heels as she left the brick-and-whitewashed stables and cantered into the pastures. Servants, including James Favour, scurried out of her way. Charlotte's tight pants clung to the fine line of her thighs and the red in her coat heightened her own natural color. Her tawny hair was concealed under her cap and only the fine high Fairchild face was visible—her voluptuous mouth bowed into a smile, the flecks in her eyes glittering. She looked fifteen years younger than she was, the most vital person there. I stood agape with the rest of them.

The men removed their caps as the minister strode into the pasture clutching a Bible and dressed in a long, black frock with lacy white surplice. The riders and spectators gathered round him under a cold but cloudless sky. The hills in the distance were laced with green and gold and the hedges everywhere were snaked with autumn flames. The men put their flasks away as the minister began with a quotation from Saint Francis, then thanked God, not just for the beauty of the world but for the beauty of our particular world—for the opulence, the wealth, the acknowledged social fabric that supported each man in his place and united these riders to these beasts. "Praised be our Lord," he intoned. He asked the responding congregation to join with him in thanking God for making us booted and spurred, co-equal with wind and water and earth—co-equal, that is, with nature and superior to everyone on foot. He assured us that God had put the horse on this earth for our pleasure so that "we might learn from his endurance, steadfastness, and contentment"; that God had put the dog on the earth for our pleasure and security and so that "we might learn from his loyalty." He even said that God had put the fox on the earth for our pleasure and "so that we might learn from his wiles." He pronounced the fox strong and smart and beautiful.

And doomed, I thought, reminded of the dining-room mural. But then the last "Amen" sounded and the horn's splendid note pierced the air and the dogs burst into furious yelping and the riders followed them out of the pasture as the spectators and servants scurried for the safety of the fences. Dolly and I were caught in a circle of jostling horse flanks, black and red jackets, the creak of leather and the crack of whips, but from the corner of my eye I saw Favour running towards Charlotte with his arms outstretched beseechingly. Her whip came down on Dancer's flank, though it was clearly intended for Favour, and Dancer bolted, throwing Favour to the ground. The last thing I saw before Dolly carried me, quite against my will, into the trees and the herd of riders, was Favour sprawled in the pasture, Marian running to help him to his feet, the silver stirrup cups spilled around him like nuggets and Charlotte galloping towards her rightful place at the head of the hunt.

9

I bounced for miles on Dolly, gripping the reins helplessly with one hand and clinging to the pommel with the other. Dolly the nag suddenly grew imperious and eager to keep up with the other riders, and it was all I could do to watch for low branches and hold on. Ahead I could see the other horses rising, high and graceful, into the air. Jumping. Great God in the morning, I thought, am I expected to jump? I could barely ride, but Dolly did the jumping—at least she bounded into the air and gravity separated my bottom from the comforting rhythmic touch of the saddle and I had to let go. For one split second I watched the gold and greenery fly by me, and then Dolly's hooves flew over me; looking up, I saw more hooves clattering towards me as I landed on the ground and rolled quickly out of the way of the last few riders, all of them young ladies, and all of whom cursed me in most unladylike fashion and rode on, desperate not to be left behind.

I lay there for a while, listening as the thud of the hooves diminished and wondering which of my extremities I'd smashed, but everything seemed to move without too much pain. I was bruised but not broken. My smart riding outfit, however, was muddied, torn, and streaked with blood that poured from my broken lip. My hat, with its black satin ribbon, and the crop were gone forever. I struggled to my feet and vainly called for Dolly, who, I found out later, had completed the chase to the very end.

I dusted myself off and began the nearly five-mile walk back to Belle Haven. I knew all the landmarks, so it was not difficult, only increasingly painful as my body began to protest the fall. I was limping badly by the time I approached the house; these were new boots, never broken in and never intended for a five-mile walk over the Virginia hills. I thought I should tell them at the stables that I'd lost Dolly, or that she'd lost me, or at the very least that she might be roaming the woods somewhere, but as I approached the tack room I could hear the raucous laughing voices of the grooms, not only Belle Haven's two stablemen, but all the other riders' grooms as well. They were clearly downing the last of the whiskey and lemon juice and I could not bring myself to announce to that group of horse fanciers that I'd fallen off the nag Dolly. Drunk or not, the grooms would of course hear me out respectfully but the minute I was out of earshot, they'd laugh themselves silly. Let Dolly take her chances in the woods, I thought irritably.

I rounded the tack room and went to the back of the stables so that no one would see me. In the days of Charles Fairchild the stables housed more than thirty fine horses, but that was long ago. Now only four horses were kept there regularly—the back rows of paddocks were vacant and weed strewn, and the brick buildings maintained only haphazardly. White paint peeled in long ribbons from the doors and the heart-shaped locks were rusted shut.

The once cloudless sky was scudded now with gray, and the wind that bore down was no longer the lilting dry breeze that had ruffled the riders' scarves earlier in the day. As I walked past the ivy-clotted walls, down the leaf-choked paths, my lip throbbed and I hoped I didn't have any more obvious bruises. How horrible it will be at the ball that evening, I thought, accepting condolences for my swollen mouth, to say nothing of my battered pride. Everyone would know I was no credit to the Fairchilds. But my heart lifted a bit when I realized that this was the first day since our awful parting that Bay Hamilton had not absorbed my every waking thought. I felt suddenly lighter.

I heard a distant moan, like the cry of a wounded animal. For one awful moment I feared it might be the fox. The muffled, piteous whining screeched, like a knife through ice, and my eyes rested uneasily on the last stall, where the heart-shaped lock hung open, broken.

I approached it uncertainly. The hinges squealed. Dank, briny, and unmistakable, the odor of vanished animals assaulted me as I peered into the gloom. It was no animal. It said, "Please go away."

"Favour," I whispered, "is that you?"

"Please," he moaned, "go away, leave me alone."

I stepped inside the cheerless damp stall, shut out from the sunlight for years. Rotting horse collars hung from the rafters and mice scurried in the feed bins. I pushed the door open a bit more to allow the murky morning light into the stall and walked over to the huddled lump of Favour, still clad in his formal butler's black, his golden head shaking with sobs.

"Favour, it's me, it's Dabney. I'm not going to hurt you." I patted his soft head as if he were a wounded animal. "It's only me. What's wrong?"

"Go away." He crouched farther into the corner and I took my hand from his head. I had never witnessed such anguish before, though I'd heard it. Once before.

"Please tell me what's wrong, Favour. Maybe I can help."

Favour brought his beautiful face up from his arms. His

long lashes were wet and tears dripped from his chin. The perfectly bowed mouth was twisted in a grimace and his eyes were awash in pain. Yet his whole expression remained vacant, as empty of understanding as a crystal goblet would be, and for the first time I realized that Favour was not simply clumsy and inexpertly obedient, but simpleminded as well, an inadequate brain set adrift in a beautiful body.

It was my turn to plead. "Please, Favour. Perhaps I can help."

"No, you can't, miss. No one can. I'm finished."

"What do you mean?"

"I can't go back. I can't! She knows that. What will happen to me, miss? I can't go back there. What will happen to me?" He broke into fresh paroxysms of weeping. "No one cares."

"I care, Favour. Tell me what happened."

"I been let go, miss. I been given my notice. I have to leave Belle Haven. I told her I'd do anything she wanted. I done everything she wanted. Everything." In the murky half light Favour paled to the color of bleached muslin and his eyes rolled back in his head. "I begged her. Let me stay at Belle Haven. I'd sleep in the stables. I wouldn't be no bother. I'd do anything she wanted. I'll be good. I will, I promise." He stared at me as if he were not quite certain to whom he was speaking. "I'm no good, miss."

"That's not true. You're a fine butler."

He clutched at my hands; his touch was cold and bony and smooth. "Not that, miss. I couldn't serve Caesar his dinner, but there's other things, things you don't understand I did and I did good. I always did what I was told, but you'd never understand."

"Please don't cry, Favour. I'll talk to Charlotte."

"She won't listen. She never does."

"I'll make her listen to me."

He regarded me with the look of disdain that the moron reserves for the cretin.

"I'll make her listen," I vowed. "I'll talk her into keeping you on, giving you another chance."

He wiped his nose on his sleeve and ran his hands through his hair. "You don't know, miss. I thought Belle Haven was heaven, but it wasn't, it was hell, hell, miss, but it was better than the last hell. Better than that. It's no good now, though. It's all up with me. They don't want me no more. They say they're tired of me. How could someone do that, miss? How could they? How could someone do that?"

Not only had I no answer for his question, I hadn't so much as a handkerchief to offer him, only the pointless promise that I would try to save his job and then, if that failed, I said that surely Charlotte would give him a reference so he could find other work. Then Favour patted my hand, as if I were the half-demented member of this duo. "Don't think I'm not grateful, miss. I'm grateful. I am. But I'm done for," he murmured. He turned his face back to the brick wall.

"How much notice did she give you?"

"Tomorrow. I have to be out tomorrow."

"Don't you worry, Favour. I'm going to make sure you don't get fired. Don't you leave tomorrow. I'll take care of everything. I promise."

"I'm grateful, miss. Don't think I'm not grateful or an unfaithful servant."

"I don't think anything of the sort." I stood and moved toward the door; in the dim light his face receded.

"You better go now, miss. They'll miss you."

Not likely, I thought ruefully. No one at Belle Haven has ever missed me, I thought, but I left him after he promised he wouldn't cry anymore, when I think I actually made him believe I might be able to sway Charlotte Courtney. The minute I stepped out of that dank paddock, however, all my confident talk struck me as ridiculous, vainglorious. Maybe I was wrong even to have given him a shred of hope that I might succeed.

The earth beneath my feet felt comforting and secure after the springy, untrustworthy floor of the paddock. The musky smell of autumn enveloped me and I resolved to do my best by Favour even if it meant standing up to my aunt and threatening her and Eugene with blackmail. As I walked towards the house, I noticed for the first time the seeping rot that encircled Belle Haven. Dusty cobwebs hung like lace in all the boxwood hedges, and elaborate spiders' webs were strung across paths where no one walked anymore. A hammock tethered to a single tree lay in the dead and dying grass. Scum rimmed the ponds, mildew had collected in the crotches and armpits of the statuary, and the dry fountains were crumbling. Everywhere the fetid excrescence of ginkgo berries tainted the air; the fallen berries, the color and texture of lifeless flesh, moldered odiferously into the ground.

How could I not have seen all this before? Summer with all its gaudy opulence and the bright banner of my love for Bay must have masked this decay, blinded my eyes. Only when the autumn winds had stripped both the trees and my love, did this corruption—root and branch—bare its fangs.

Random shots from hunters in the distant woods rang out; nearer by, the smell of woodsmoke floated past. I made my way through the boxwood mazes, past the stone Diana until I came to the sculpted cherub, bound hand and foot with a garland of roses, where, as if under some wicked enchantment, I suddenly stopped and stared. The cherub's expression was exactly like that of the man I'd just left. As with Favour, his beauty was brutalized and his features contorted as only the uncomprehending can suffer. And through all the years between me and that fateful autumn I can see that face before me still. I knew even then that, in some as yet inscrutable way, Favour was doomed. That Belle Haven was doomed. That I was doomed too, though I did not know by what or by whom.

10

Though the salon was ablaze with electric lights, silver candelabra had been placed strategically about to heighten reflections in the mirrors, to flatter the pearly skin of the women guests, to shine on the portraits of the four Fairchild beauties who presided over the ball.

"Dabney dear! Come here!" Charlotte's voice blew across the salon like an ill wind. She stood beneath her own portrait, thinner now, less relaxed, clad in a backless beaded dress of herbal green velvet spangled with silver. She looked like a thornless rose, but I knew better. "Come over here, Dabney, I want you to meet someone."

I excused myself from Dr. and Mrs. Pruitt and their dull inquiries into my broken lip and made my way through the rustling silks of the women and the stiff-pressed evening clothes of the men. My own dress was a watered silk of midnight blue with a sleeveless tunic of pale lace. It was the first truly adult evening dress I'd ever worn, and as I passed Eugene I even elicited a jaded compliment from him. "You ought to display your shoulders more frequently, Dabney. And midnight blue becomes you. It goes with your bruises." I blushed and cringed at the same instant. Sensing my discomfort, Eugene laughed, lit a cigarette, and walked away.

It took me some time to make my way to Charlotte. Three times as many people attended the ball as had come to the hunt. They gathered like extravagantly colored sea urchins in little tidal pools surrounding the champagne and canapés, awash in horsey conversation.

"Ah, here she is, Mr. Emery. My niece, Dabney Antonia Beale," Charlotte announced.

"Miss Beale," said the vapid-looking Mr. Emery. He bowed stiffly from the waist as if, I reflected irreverently, he were in need of a lube job.

"I'm trying to marry my niece off, Mr. Emery," Charlotte said coolly, "though it will be difficult now that everyone here knows she can't ride."

"Were you hurt in your fall, Miss Beale? Your lip is quite swollen."

"No," I grunted.

"Would you like to marry my niece, Mr. Emery? She's not an exciting conversationalist, as you may have gathered, and she's rather moody of late, but she plays the piano like an angel."

"I'd love to hear you play sometime, Miss Beale."

"I'm not marrying anyone, Charlotte."

"I fear you're right, Dabney." She sighed and turned her captivating smile on Mr. Emery. "You'd have to teach her manners as well as riding, Mr. Emery. I'm afraid she isn't much of a catch, for all her money."

For all her money? I colored deeply and the flustered Mr. Emery was rescued by the orchestra, which filled the salon with the strains of a popular sad waltz. He asked Charlotte to dance with him and she slid into his arms and glided away.

I backed into a convenient corner where I could see Favour, who stood like a martinet beside the French doors leading into the hall. A visibly shaken martinet. His lips had a bluish tint and he regarded the party with unseeing eyes.

He had probably been told to stand there as he could not have been trusted with trays of champagne, particularly not with all the dancers swirling about the room. That task was left to the imported servants, who were graceful and mute.

Marian, who was mute but not graceful, stood at attention behind the silver punch bowl filled with the Gentlemen's Punch, more of the whiskey and sugar and lemon juice ("And prohibition be damned!"). She served the gentlemen so they would not soil their white gloves with a drop of the pungent brew. Austin—rather like Marian—never left his post beside the punch bowl. On his best behavior, he filled his own cup copiously and often and watched the party with wobbling eyes and a look of evident satisfaction. Sometimes he talked to the men who came to the punch bowl, but they never lingered. Punctilious, polite to Austin, they wandered elsewhere to be convivial.

Eugene surveyed the Belle Haven ball from a post near the piano. He sipped champagne and carried on a conversation with three or four people, his eyes constantly darting over their heads, making certain that nothing escaped his notice. Not even me. The slight crinkling of his lips indicated a smile, but I looked away.

A group of late arrivals burst through the door, brushing past Favour with a medley of vivacious chatter about a car breaking down and a ride on a hay wagon. A half dozen of them, four men and two women, entered together. At the center I recognized Marjorie Vail (Merrywell, Class of Nineteen). She was smaller than she had appeared on horseback, arrayed in a gown that was sashed and fluted with gold brocade. Her eyes never left the French doors, though she leaned pliantly towards one of the young men and chided him for exaggeration. Suddenly her face lit up—and through the French doors came Bay Hamilton.

Unbidden, all the passion he'd ever aroused in me ignited, and I felt I had to crash through the crowd into his arms, except that Marjorie Vail sailed into those arms and bent her fair head to his shoulder, whispering towards his ear. His arm encircled her back and he led her to the dance floor. I, quaking, abashed, horrified, sank against the marble fireplace, where I tried to recover my dignity or melt into the marble—whichever came first. Over Marjorie's head Bay looked for me, and when his eyes met mine I moved closer to the fire and fought with rage and love and loss, each emotion all-consuming, and I thought I could smell my illusions burning all around me. I scarcely noticed Eugene moving coolly across the floor towards me. I pushed him away when he gripped my shoulders, but his bony hands were firm and he pulled me from the fireplace and poured champagne on my smoking hem. More than my illusions had burned. The edge of my dress had caught fire. It was ruined.

"So that's how it is, eh, Dabney?" He chuckled. "I should have guessed that our little summer butterfly got her wings from a man."

"You disgust me, Eugene."

"And you are beginning to intrigue me, Dabney."

"You have a low mind."

The rattle of polite applause signaled the end of the dance and suddenly I was the center of attention, surrounded by people bemoaning the scorching of my dress. Charlotte and Mr. Emery returned to us and Eugene announced that I thought I was Joan of Arc. Charlotte explained to one and all that I always was a clumsy child and not to be trusted near fire. I felt like the rose-bound cherub, in excruciating pain and unable to escape; when Mr. Emery offered me a glass of champagne I took it without comment and downed it in one hasty gulp, because Marjorie Vail was leading Bay Hamilton right for us.

Bay never took his eyes from mine. He looked pale and thin. Tired. I longed to snatch Marjorie Vail's possessive hand from his arm. O my beloved. Love is strong as death; jealousy is cruel as the grave. My lost, my lake, lover. Had he made a woman of the girl Marjorie Vail as he had made a woman out of Dabney Beale? I wished to God that I were a girl again, a little girl who could hide behind the skirt encircling a sink and not be found for ages.

I scarcely heard Marjorie Vail, but her lilting, inbred Virginia accent tripped lightly over her excuses. ". . . And I just know that my dress was ruined riding in the back of the hay wagon, but what else could we do? I told Bay, I wouldn't miss one of Belle Haven's hunt balls for anything and if Charlotte doesn't understand that we had to bring a plowhorse to her door, why then she just doesn't know how highly esteemed her parties are. And Bay, oh Charlotte, forgive my manners. I declare, I clean forgot in all the excitement. Let me present my"—her sharp little features were galvanized in a moment of faked anxiety—"my escort, Dr. Bay Hamilton. Bay's been visiting Daddy on some dreary old business or another—by the way, Charlotte, Daddy sends his regrets. He's not well, you know, but now with Bay looking after him I'm sure he'll be his old self any day now. But anyway, I just thought I'll ask Bay to come to the Hunt Ball and Charlotte won't mind. The more the merrier, that's what I always say."

"That's not always true," said Charlotte in a voice that had the ring of carbon steel.

"Well, of course it's not always true, but it usually is, isn't that so, Bay? Dr. Hamilton's just returned to Oakstone this year, Charlotte. He was with our gallant forces in France and he was wounded, too—didn't you say you were wounded, Bay?"

My gaze strayed to Bay's right thigh. Wounded and the stitches removed clumsily so that I could trace the scar with my fingers and had traced it with my fingers and had moved my fingers up . . .

". . . After France and Johns Hopkins, why, I'm just sure Dr. Hamilton finds Virginia dull as dishwater, but I told him, well, there's one person here who isn't the least bit dull and that is Charlotte Courtney and you just have to come meet her."

"We've met."

"And this is Mr. Duckworth and Charlotte's niece Daphne—you've met?"

"We've all met."

"At one time or another," Eugene said, shifting his eyes momentarily to me.

Bay stared at Charlotte as if she were a test tube to which he was adding some incalculable fluid. "Mrs. Courtney and I are old friends. We have been for years. Ever since she was married to my father. My dead father."

"Oh Lordy." Marjorie broke out in a visible sweat. "I clean forgot about—"

"He committed suicide when he was married to Mrs. Courtney," Bay went on, coldly ignoring Marjorie's confusion. "You know the type—he preferred death to dishonor. Married to her he'd had such a long taste of dishonor that he reckoned death couldn't be much worse."

"Why look," Marjorie cried "there's Emmalee Frazier. I haven't seen Emmalee in a coon's age. You'll just have to excuse Bay and me, Charlotte, Mr. Duckworth, Daphne."

"Dabney."

"Yes, well, come on, Bay."

"You go, Marjorie. I want a few words with Mrs. Courtney about some documents she promised me. She said I could have them and I've come to collect."

"I never said any such thing," Charlotte said with steely conviction.

The quailing Marjorie vanished, Mr. Emery slunk away, and the three of us—Charlotte, Eugene, and I—stood before Bayard Hamilton, rooted to the parquet floor beneath our feet, each hating him for different reasons.

"Have you reconsidered my request, Mrs. Courtney?"

Eugene stepped between them as if he expected a fistfight. "I've told you repeatedly, Dr. Hamilton, every time you've come to my office and I've been good enough to see you; I've told you the same thing. You don't seem to listen."

"No, Duckworth, you don't seem to hear. I've told you that I intend to get these documents from Mrs. Courtney, and until I do, none of us will have any peace."

"Mrs. Courtney is under no obligation to relinquish any of your late father's effects, if indeed there were any such effects, which there aren't."

"No? Not even a suicide note? I want that note for my mother, who is a dying woman."

"Mrs. Courtney—" Eugene began, but Charlotte interrupted him.

"Really, Eugene, let's not be tiresome with Dr. Hamilton. Can't you see we're supposed to be awed by his filial devotion? I for one am awed, I confess. Dr. Hamilton, you have simply bowled me over with your filial devotion." The treacle in her voice was belied by the menace she exuded, more pungent than Rappaccini cologne. "But we all know how this is going to end, don't we, Dr. Hamilton? Your mother will die and she will die without ever laying her hands on her errant husband's trashy effects. Dr. Hamilton will congratulate himself for having done the right thing by her, for having gallantly tried, as a good son should, to fill his mother's last wish. And gallantly failed."

"I do not fail gallantly, Mrs. Courtney."

"I'll bet you don't," she said, a queer half smile lighting her face. "But between failure and morning there's always tonight, and tonight the dictates of hospitality require that I treat you civilly. But don't underestimate me. Don't ever underestimate me. If, after tonight, you so much as set foot on Belle Haven property, I'll set Caesar on you. I'll shoot you on sight. Do I make myself clear? I have a gun, Dr.

Hamilton, and I know how to use it and I shall happily, happily use it on you. Now come, Eugene." She took his arm. "Let's get away from all this vermin cluttering the floor," and they swept into the swirl of dancers.

Bay stared at me, his eyes clouded with defeat. For everything I longed to say, I was suddenly speechless, but slowly the words formed on my lips, whispered to the mocking counterpoint of music and laughter. "She means it," I began.

"You look beautiful tonight, Dabney," he replied as if he had not heard me.

"Charlotte would shoot you."

"You look beautiful and I've missed you."

"Liar. You got what you wanted from me. Some sort of private revenge for—"

"That's not true. I've told you what's true, that no matter how much we love each other—"

"I don't love you, I don't."

"Dabney—there's no future—not when we have to contend with the past—"

"Don't talk to me about the past! I hate the past. I despise it and I despise you and I'll never forgive you."

"I don't ask your forgiveness."

"But you wanted my love, didn't you?"

"Not at first. I never intended—"

"Oh, spare me your noble intentions, you hypocrite. You're worse than Charlotte—at least she doesn't pretend to be noble. You! You used me and now you show up with that simpering ninny, that twit."

"Marjorie Vail can't help what she is."

"Oh my," I said with a sarcastic inflection reminiscent of Charlotte, "how perfectly gentlemanly of you. You and all your talk of death and dishonor."

"I love you, Dabney."

"You took everything I had and when you were done—"

"Not everything. I left you your virginity, don't forget." He smiled ironically as if his little joke gave him enormous pleasure.

His eyes traveled over me in a way that made me feel we were once again in that dawn-lit crumbling boathouse; he stirred all the old naked impulses, the damp desires, as though I stood before him stripped, hungry, and hot. I drew my hand back and slapped his face so hard his skin cracked and my hand burned with pain.

The slap sounded like a shot fired into the salon and everything seemed to halt—dancers, laughter, conversation; the very champagne ceased to fizzle in the glasses and for one drawn and quartered second Bay and I stared grimly at each other.

He put his hand to his cheek. "That's a nasty cut on your lip, Dabney." He turned away from me, into the rescuing arms of Marjorie Vail—who had flown across the room, as had Austin, who stood panting at my side, demanding to know what this was all about. "Has he offended you, Dabney? Should I pluck out his eye? I'll challenge him—" Austin cried pugnaciously. Mr. Emery appeared from nowhere and Austin pushed Emery into my arms, commanding us to dance. The band quickly struck up a fast, lively tune and I was whirled out amidst the flashing jewels and sparkling lights. Over Mr. Emery's shoulder I could see all of them watching me: Favour with his cold, troubled eyes; Charlotte's face puckered with curiosity and surprise (two emotions she never expressed); Eugene eyeing me with intense reptilian interest; and Marjorie Vail regarding me as if I were a mismatched cup and saucer set. And Bay, oh yes, Bay too, but I refused to meet his eyes. They all stared at me with what I intuitively recognized was fear: they were afraid of me. Indeed, I was afraid of myself. They knew and I knew that in some way I held their mingled fates in my inexperienced, impulsive hands.

People made certain that Bay Hamilton and I were apart

the rest of the evening. My act had given this party an almost palpable dimension of raw gossip and delight. I drank champagne and listened to rumblings all around me, the old scandal of Charlotte and Dr. Hamilton raked up, reconstituted, in furtive whispers. Charlotte looked positively ashen and when supper was announced I saw Marjorie Vail take her aside, clutch at her arm, and mutter apologies all over again. Charlotte turned to her with an arctic glare, peeled Marjorie's fingers from her arm, and left Marjorie in her wake the way an ocean liner leaves a tugboat behind.

For supper, the guests (some much debilitated by a day of hard drinking and riding, and a night of hard drinking and dancing) filed into the dining room, where the buffet table was spread beneath the mural. Six smoking clove-studded hams were carved by an imported butler who flourished his knives with the expertise of a surgeon. Other servants, equally skillful, dissected two dozen ducks cooked to a mahogany brown and three huge turkeys that lay on huge silver platters. Several roast loins of pork oozed hazelnut stuffing, vegetables in aspic quivered across the table beside mounds of sweet potatoes, the butter running down their slopes. On the sideboard were the desserts: pumpkin soufflés, a dozen symmetrical apple tarts, carmelized pears standing upright in lakes of cream, and four baked Alaskas. All of it—the gleaming silver, the flaxen napery, the fragrances, design, decor— was guaranteed to excite the senses, and in the midst of all this prodigal abundance stood Charlotte Courtney, undisputed mistress of her domain, sullied by an ancient scandal, humiliated by a country doctor, shamed by an impulsive niece. Her eyes exactly matched the eyes of the fox in the mural behind her and I reflected momentarily that my father must have known her well to have captured that look.

I admired her, I admit it. Cringing with the mortification I'd brought on myself, I could not help but admire Charlotte's assured aplomb. Of course one should never confess to admiring the depraved, but I admired her just the same. Admired her and loathed her. Just as I loved and loathed Bay. And now, looking back on it, I can see that on the night of the Belle Haven ball, I was initiated into the adult world. The passion, the awakened hungers, the carnal knowledge I'd learned with Bay that summer had all made of me a woman. But that night I was introduced to adult confusions, the irrefutable twine-and-vine of contradiction: beauty and depravity, abundance and waste, awe and disgust, high principles and low expedience, lies rooted in truth, hate rooted in love.

"Charlotte's quite a woman, isn't she?" Austin came up behind me, reeking of punch and Cuban cigars. "No matter what she's done—though God knows all and God will punish the wicked," he added in an afterbreath, "there isn't a woman here, or a man either for that matter, who's her equal. 'Who is she that looketh forth as the morning, fair as the moon, clear as the sun and terrible as an army with banners?' 'O the prince's daughter, the joints of her thighs are like jewels.' She taketh away my breath, Dabney, I declare, she does. There isn't another human being like her."

"Thank God for that."

"Do not take God's name in vain, Dabney."

"I wasn't, Austin. I meant to thank Him."

Austin supported himself against the wainscoting. "What did that young man say to you, Dabney? Did he impugn your honor? A nice girl like you—you would never slap anyone, Dabney. Why did you? Shall I call him forth as a cad?"

"Please—Austin, never mind."

"I'm ready to stand in defense of your honor, Dabney."

"I know, Austin, dear Austin, thank you, but it's quite all right."

"It doesn't seem to be."

He regarded me quizzically, but I left his side before he

could question me further. I filled my plate and returned to the salon, where small tables had been set up all over the dance floor. I shared my supper uncomfortably with Mr. Emery, Dr. and Mrs. Pruitt, one or two other thickly up-holstered matrons, and an old man with liver-spotted hands. They were suddenly all very interested in me. They wanted to know how long I had been at Belle Haven and when I intended to return to Merrywell College. When I told them I had been expelled from Merrywell for taking a cow into the library, they shut up. The ladies excused themselves to go upstairs and refresh their coiffures and their fading fra-grances (or, more likely, to have a cigarette; Charlotte was the only one with enough courage to smoke in front of men). Dr. Pruitt, Mr. Emery, and Mr. Liverspot retreated to the library, no doubt in search of a box of cigars and a decanter of brandy. I was left alone. I thought perhaps I could make my escape unobtrusively—only Favour guarded the French doors. I went up to him and patted his shoulder lightly. "I haven't talked to Charlotte yet, Favour, but I will. I know I can talk her into keeping you on. Don't you leave tomorrow, Favour. I'm going to take care of everything."

He brought his blue eyes up to me; they were expression-less, cold as silver dollars. "Don't bother, miss."

"Nonsense, Favour, I'm going to do it."

"You will waste your breath, miss. She will be angry with you, too."

An inebriated gentleman asked to be shown the way to the library and Favour obliged him. I darted into the hall and out the front doors for a breath of air that was my own. I wandered aimlessly down the long drive under a pregnant orange moon and the half-clad branches of the dogwood trees, their dry, blood red leaves rustling in the wind. I stood at the bottom of the drive, listening to the water trickle in the muddy creek below and gazing through the open gates at the highway. I half believed that if I took but one step, the road would do the rest, carry me far, far from Belle Haven, from shame, from the ubiquitous past.

But nothing of the sort happened. The night was cold and I was sleeveless and shivering and suddenly exhausted, as if slapping Bay had burst my awful apprehension. At last I knew I could sleep; my body and mind begged for deep, dreamless sleep. My having slapped Bay in full view of the Belle Haven ball had stripped from me my last vestige of pride, but oddly, my sense of loss was leavened by a brisk, invigorating sense of freedom.

I returned to the house and peered into the salon through the window. Bay and Marjorie Vail were nowhere to be seen and indeed the party seemed to have thinned considerably. Many of the men were drunk and the women so languid as to appear wilted. The orchestra was off key and the candles sputtered low, leaving little petals of wax on the furniture. Even Charlotte looked tired, though Eugene's eyes seemed brighter than I remembered. Poor Austin had passed out by the piano and everyone politely stepped around him with the interest they might have donated to a pothole in the road.

I went round to the servants' entrance and took the servants' stairwell up to my room. I threw open the window to blow out the smell of powdered shoulders and cigarette smoke the women guests had left in my room. As I pulled off my scorched midnight blue gown, some of the seams gave way. I didn't care. I'd never wear it again. I kicked off my shoes and, clad only in my underwear, I tumbled into bed and the soothing bliss of sleep, tortured only briefly by a longing to feel Bay's skin beneath my fingers again. Whether in a slap or caress, it no longer mattered which.

11

As dawn crept into my room I rolled over in bed and groaned. My body ached, my head throbbed, my brain, it seemed, had sprouted mildew and my tongue had sprouted fur. I was well into the throes of my first hangover. Last night's wonderful sense of freedom had fled and in its place was the awful realization that I would have to find, fabricate, or cobble together some explanation of my behavior at the ball. Charlotte would never let it lie. She would have it out of me and what could I say? I slapped Bay Hamilton because he made a disparaging remark about you, Charlotte dear. That would never do. And Eugene—the thought of his prying gaze made me positively nauseated. More nauseated than I already was. I made my way to the bathtub, where by turns I parboiled myself in hot water and froze myself with cold. I dried myself quickly, brushed my hair out, and then wound it in a penitent's knot at my neck. I could not think properly in the confines of my room and I knew as I pulled on wool stockings, my still-muddied riding pants, boots, and a thick sweater that I would have to go to the lake. I would stay there until I came up with a suitable story, which, I reflected grimly, could take me days.

I made my way cautiously out to the landing, where bits of conversation—an animated and still-drunken political argument—floated upwards. No need to fear an encounter with Eugene if there were recalcitrant guests still here. I used the servants' staircase nonetheless and as I crept by the kitchen I could hear Ethel's unmistakable voice cursing Favour. "Damnation, Marian, where is he? You're always covering up for him. I'll find the little bloodsucker and give it to him with the rolling pin, I will. I'll see he loses his job. Two hours' sleep and I'm expected to serve breakfast and clean up this unholy mess with the help of nothing but a bunch of witless mutes and the dimmest wit of all nowhere to be found. Now then, Marian, where is he?" Without waiting for an answer Ethel launched into another spray of invective. "What am I supposed to say to Mrs. Courtney? Begging your pardon, madame, but you can't expect me to run a house with that Favour for a butler and him never around when you need him, the little rat. Clumsy as a one-legged turkey he is and stupid besides. When I find him I'm going to pin his ears to his skull. You wait and see what I do to Mr. Favour!"

I darted past the kitchen as quickly as I could and out the backdoor, where the cold overcast morning air eased my aching head. I longed to escape the house and Ethel, who, I felt, had implicated me in her tirade. Guilt by association— as if I too were shirking my duties.

I ran through the boxwood maze, without so much as a glance at the rose-bound cherub or the eager Diana, past the stinking ginkgo trees, and down into the woods, with their autumn odors of drying lichen and dying leaves. Tiny ornaments of red and gold decorated the bittersweet hedges and brilliant wild persimmons dotted the trees; the huge cedars dripped amber sap. The Virginia autumn was working itself into a splendid crescendo and then it would crash into one last, long chord, the prelude to winter.

As I came to the lake a family of wild geese burst from

the rushes and took to the sky. Clamoring birds swirled overhead, seeking the distant treetops, and were roosting there noisily as I ran towards the rotting boathouse. At the dock only two boats were tied. I nearly cried out with joy: Bay was here, he'd taken the third boat. I scanned the lake, though I saw nothing. He must have rowed out where the lake made its slight northward curl, just beyond my sight. I snapped the *Francesca*'s oars from the boathouse wall and got in, tempted to call his name even then, tempted to spill to the lake and the trees, to the world itself, my joy: Bay had been driven here too. The hangover, the evil crust imprisoning me from the night before, peeled away like the bark off a sycamore. The physical act of rowing refreshed me, the wind ruffled my hair, and the *Francesca* slid effortlessly over the pewter gray water, the dipping oars chanting *Bay Bay Bay.*

But, when I rounded the lake's gentle bend, the empty *Charlotte* bobbed forlornly into view. The oars were tucked neatly into the oarlocks, but the boat was deserted and the still, chill water held no swimmer. "Bay," I called out, "Bay!" and my voice, carried by the wind, echoed off the trees. I stopped rowing and held the oars tightly. "Hello!" I cried and overhead the birds broke into a frenzy of flight and raucous cawing. "Is anyone here? Hello?" Only the birds and wind responded and slowly I rowed nearer the *Charlotte,* where the water had turned an odd cast of sepia and lavender, as if it had been badly bruised. As I pulled up near the empty boat, my breath constricted and I burst into sweat that prickled along my scalp and back and behind my knees and I blubbered out, "Oh Lord, protect me," because the bright yellow paint I had so carefully applied last spring was mottled with splashes of still-fresh scarlet across the seats, the floor, the narrow hull. Blood. And beneath the empty boat, a rust-colored plume spread. As I dipped my oars into that ghastly brew and the *Francesca* nudged the *Charlotte,* she bobbed away from me, just out of reach, and revealed a black-clad creature floating face down and limp in the water, arms out-stretched as if beseeching me. Blood billowed from what had once been the golden-thatched skull of James Favour.

After that, Belle Haven erupted, besieged by the sheriff, the coroner, the county hearse, the county attorney, all the official midwives of death and disaster. The serenity of my lake was forever shattered by the sheriff's crew of volunteers who brought James Favour in and then—ghastly thought—dove into the bloody waters to recover the gun with which he'd killed himself.

Gawkers, onlookers, black, white, the respectable, the ne-farious, the merely no-account, they all descended on Belle Haven Lake to watch this grisly process. They came from as near as Oakstone and as far away as Lynchburg. They tram-pled through the woods and wandered the boxwood mazes with impunity, as if the suicide of one lowly butler decreed Belle Haven public, the property of any who cared to come, watch, be horrified or amused.

No one came to mourn, I can tell you that. The sheriff and the county coroner wanted to ask Charlotte if James Favour had any next of kin and where he had come from, but, on Dr. Pruitt's orders, Charlotte was sedated and not required to answer anything. Eugene was left to deal with a situation that, rather like the lake itself, grew more murky the more people dived into it.

Eugene said it was not his custom to inquire into the back-ground of Mrs. Courtney's servants and directed them to Ethel, who swore she knew nothing. Ethel claimed James Favour simply appeared one day in Mrs. Courtney's tow and was announced to Ethel as the new butler. Gradually it was established that Favour had arrived at Belle Haven with Mrs. Courtney after one of her trips to New York and that, beyond that, nothing was known of him. The body waited in the county morgue for ten days while they searched in vain for a relative of any sort. Finally Eugene told the coroner to bury James Favour and send the bill to Belle Haven.

The funeral was sparsely attended—only the servants and me. Eugene claimed urgent business, though he sent a wreath. Charlotte was still under Dr. Pruitt's care and Austin was too drunk to go. Then there was the coroner's inquest.

Everyone at Belle Haven was required to appear and testify. We shivered in the barren, unheated courtroom and faced the judge's elevated bench, where he sat flanked by flags with Latin mottos. The judge, who had attended the hunt and the Belle Haven ball, was a florid middle-aged man with bushy gray hair and weak eyes who studied his own fleshy hands throughout the proceedings. He had closed the hearing to all but the participants, so we were spared the gaping, curious crowd.

Ethel gave a rather more moderate version of the speech I'd overheard in the kitchen that morning, noting only that after the party she could not find Mr. Favour anywhere. The other servants concurred that they had last seen him the night of the ball. They said he was timid and had not made any friends. He had apparently left no note and they were shocked he would take his own life.

The district attorney called Marian to the stand. She looked as slovenly as ever, in a man's heavy sweater, pockets bulging with scraps of paper and the chewed stubs of pencils. She took the oath and got out a bit of paper and pencil. The clerk was required to read her testimony as she wrote it. Marian said she had not known Favour well, but that she felt sorry for him.

"And why was that?" asked the county attorney, a young man, still raw from some dismal downstate law school.

Marian touched her hair repeatedly as she shook her head.

"She means he was dimwitted, Your Honor," Ethel piped up.

"Please leave the witness to answer her own questions,"

said the judge. Then he turned to Marian. "You must be more specific. You understand?"

Marian then testified as best her grammatical skills allowed her that Favour was friendless and clumsy and seemingly had no idea of his duties, that he had had to be instructed even in the smallest of them. She added that on the day of the hunt he was at first agitated and then panic stricken, and she tried to tell how Favour had run after Charlotte when she was mounted and ready for the hunt, but all this was too much literary effort for Marian and the judge advised the young county attorney to get on with it and just ask the defendant simple yes and no questions.

"The day before his death did you notice anything unusual about Mr. Favour?"

Marian nodded excitedly and wrote haltingly that Favour had been crying.

"You know that for a fact?"

Marian held up her hand like she was ready to take the oath all over again. The county attorney excused her shortly after that, but before she left the stand she scribbled one more note and handed it to the clerk.

"No note," the clerk read out, "couldn't read or write."

"Mr. Favour was illiterate?" asked the attorney, and Marian nodded.

They tried to put Austin on the stand, but he was quickly excused because he only blubbered and ranted on about Sodom and Gomorrah and the Last Judgment and blood blood blood, blood upon us, blood being shed, waters turned to blood, the earth disclosing blood. Austin was useless. Eugene instructed the chauffeur to take him back to Belle Haven and return later for the rest of us.

Charlotte took the stand looking crisp and inviolate, discreetly mournful in a gray wool suit with a black silk blouse. She wore a black hat with a long feather that threatened to tickle the attorney's nose every time she bent her head—

which was often. Not quite crying. She didn't stoop to that, but she was clearly moved and saddened. She asked the court how could such a thing have happened at Belle Haven. They always took such good care of their servants.

The county attorney was gentle with Charlotte, respectful in fact, but he felt it his duty to inquire if she knew why James Favour appeared upset the day of the hunt.

"I do not delve into my servants' private lives, sir."

"Some of the testimony we've heard indicates that the deceased was"—the attorney stared at the defunct courtroom stove while he sought the correct phrase—"often not competent, that he was clumsy—an altogether inadequate butler."

"Are we here to judge the dead man's job performance?" replied Charlotte archly.

"No, Mrs. Courtney, but I would not think that you would introduce such a butler into your home and keep him on in the face of such blatant incompetence."

"I am surrounded by incompetence, sir. You've seen my husband, have you not? And look, look at Marian there—would a competent maid dress like Marian? Look at her stockings—they don't even match and she's got a gravy stain on her skirt. Is that competence? I keep Marian on from a sense of loyalty. We are always loyal."

"Your cook has testified that you brought James Favour back with you from New York last spring."

"That's true."

"And that you introduced him to the staff as the new butler."

"Yes?"

"Well, Mrs. Courtney, why would you have chosen such a man for a butler? Did he have references? Where did you find him?"

"A dear friend of mine in New York, Lady Rose Trevor, was returning to England and begged me to take him on. She was afraid of what would happen to him if he were left in

New York without employment. I never dreamed he was so clumsy."

"But surely you saw him when he worked for Lady Rose Trevor."

The slightest ripple of confusion marred Charlotte's brow. She was not accustomed to being caught in her own lies. "Lady Trevor and I are not in the habit of commenting upon the servants' performance. He seemed useful enough to me. Indeed, I think the servants have quite exaggerated his clumsiness and I honestly fail to see where this line of questioning is relevant to the poor man's death. He's dead—can it matter whether I—whether any of us thought him competent? He was a faithful servant to me. What else can a mistress ask of her servant?"

Charlotte offered this without the slightest flinch or blush and the judge nodded in agreement with her. I marveled at her coolness and despised her for it. The young attorney, however, was only partially defeated: there was the matter of the gun Favour had killed himself with. He established that it was Charlotte's own gun. How had Favour come by it?

Charlotte professed not to know. She explained that she had had three hundred people in her house that night and Favour could have pilfered the gun at almost any time—that night or before—without detection.

"Pilfered the gun from where?" asked the attorney.

Beside me I could feel Eugene stiffen, as if the hair in his ears and nose stood on end. On the stand, Charlotte studied the lace edge of her handkerchief.

"Where did you keep the gun, Mrs. Courtney?"

"In the desk in the library. Second drawer on the left."

Her precision seemed to satisfy the attorney and Eugene relaxed. I thought it more likely that Charlotte kept that gun in her bedroom, possibly right by the bed. Possibly in it.

My conjectures were punctured by the sound of my own

name. I rose and took the stand. The judge peered at me over a pair of thick bifocals. There was some discussion about my being a minor, but the point was set aside because this was an informal hearing and, besides, I was the one who had found the body.

As I placed my hand on the Bible and swore to tell the truth, I was ready to bring Belle Haven down in disgrace, to be faithful to such truth, or to such portion of the truth as I knew. But when the questions were asked me, I could not. I perjured my soul. Worse, my perjury was uninstructed. No one had bid me lie or threatened me if I didn't lie. And I did not precisely lie: I told only what I had seen, the body in the lake (and no one questioned what I was doing there at that early hour), but I did not tell what I knew: that James Favour had ceased to please, or satisfy, or perhaps merely intrigue his mistress, that that mistress and her lawyer lover had found him in a brothel, that his previous occupation had nothing to do with the mythical Lady Rose Trevor, that the acts he performed clumsily in public were compensated for by acts he performed gracefully in private, in my aunt's bedchamber. I said nothing of the sort. Why? Not to protect Charlotte or Eugene or even poor James Favour, who was beyond all human protection. To protect myself perhaps. After all, Favour's death at least had the merit of obscuring any questions into my own conduct the night of the Belle Haven ball. Perhaps not to protect at all. As my testimony continued and I spilled my half vial of truth, I wished I could recant, retract my misstatements, but I continued as I had begun. My voice did not betray me. I answered the questions put to me simply and without elaboration. I kept my eyes on Charlotte and Eugene. Charlotte seemed bored, impatient, but Eugene's long gray jaw had tightened visibly and he never took his eyes off me. Not once. And when I finished, he smiled—a sort of smile, anyway, a look of triumph that made me feel irrevocably tarnished.

When we got back into the car, Charlotte snapped open her bag, took out a silver flask, and had a few good belts of Canadian whiskey. She offered us each some. Eugene refused. I didn't. I needed it.

"Thank God that's over," she said, lapsing back against the upholstered cushions.

I did not contradict her, but I knew it was not over. Not for me anyway. I turned away from Charlotte and Eugene. I stared out the window. I knew that whatever corruption had tainted Belle Haven, I was not immune to it; indeed, because of my perjury I was forever implicated in it. But I could not have known—as we sped glumly, wordlessly, through the drear autumnal landscape—that James Favour's dismal end would suck me into a vortex of dead passion and depravity from which I never fully escaped.

12

Favour's death was officially declared a suicide. He was buried, and life should have gone on, but something prickly and ugly still tainted the very air at Belle Haven. The day after the hearing Charlotte was on the phone to Dr. Pruitt demanding that he prescribe something for Austin that would shut him up. Austin had not been sober since James Favour was found in the lake. The more Austin drank, the more he blathered: Sodom, Gomorrah, the greater damnation awaiting us all, corrupt trees bringing forth corrupt fruit, the fire next time, the wages of sin, and so on.

"I want you to bring it to Belle Haven and administer it yourself!" Charlotte declared. "And I don't care who's dying of what. I can't endure Austin another moment!" She slammed down the phone without so much as a goodbye and then screamed for Marian, who slouched in. "Go upstairs and pack my things. I'm getting out of here." Then she called Eugene and made arrangements to meet him at the Oakstone station, and within the hour her suitcases were loaded in the car and she was pulling on her gloves. "Be a good girl, Dabney," she said to me on her way out the door, "and don't find any more dead bodies in the lake."

This was a wasted injunction. I had not been to the lake since that day nor had I any wish to return. For the first few days after Charlotte's departure, the weather was good and I took long walks through the woods, and once I even cautiously rode Dolly as far as Oakstone, alternately hoping and fearful that I would meet Bay Hamilton. These high bright days passed quickly, though, and when the cold rains of November set in, I was imprisoned in the house with Austin, who (despite what Dr. Pruitt may have given him) remained drunk louder and longer than I could remember.

Rather than chance an encounter with Austin in the library, I took armloads of books up to my room and read there, drinking one pot of tea after another, which Marian was kind enough to bring to me. But a merely closed door is never enough to ward off a garrulous drunk, and one afternoon Austin rolled into my room, clutching a whiskey bottle, and sat on the floor in front of the fire. Quite oblivious of me, he rambled obsessively about death and the redemption of Christ.

His fiery monologue beat a dreary counterpoint to the rain pelting the windows and so I took my book and tiptoed toward the door. I had my hand on the crystal heart-shaped knob when Austin shifted his focus (if such it can be called) from the Bible to Belle Haven and I stopped and returned to the fire.

". . . Favour wasn't alone. There's been others. Lots of others. Lots of death and love. Love"—he sighed. "Love? No! Filth! Abominations! Whoredom and wine smite the heart, destroy the soul and body. The body. The body. Take my body, which is—Oh Charlotte, Charlotte," he beseeched the fire, "how could you? You loved me, Charlotte. What did I do to destroy that love? I am innocent. It was you—you drove me mad with longing, Charlotte, thy lips and tongue swept over my body like fire. Oh Charlotte—thy body is like unto a whited sepulchre, a marble sepulchre, and I have been a fool, yea—before Christ I repent of my sins and my foolishness—but I am not a madman. Not mad like that poor bastard before me. Not mad enough to kill myself."

"Favour?"

"Favour? No. Not mad enough to kill myself like the other one, not mad enough to kill myself like him. You don't love me, Charlotte. You never did. You've loved none of them, only loved what you could do to them and what they—we—would do for you. And I would do anything. Have done anything and now you don't love me." He began to weep.

"What poor bastard?" I inquired.

Austin regarded me for the first time. "Why, that poor upright dead bastard of a doctor, of course. She never loved him, either. She seduced him only to prove it could be done. She'd have me prostrate with desire and then she'd whisper to me how men were so weak, how they were ever the slaves of their bodies. There's no man who can't be seduced, Austin, she'd whisper along my spine, and I said yes, yes, and then she said, no man who can't be seduced no matter what his pretensions to loyalty or respectability. Men are such soft, malleable creatures, Austin—and then she'd knead my flesh with her fingers and I said yes and yes and then she said she could prove it and I took her in my arms and said, prove it by me, Charlotte, prove it by me. But she told me how she proved it with her other lovers, legions of them, men she despised, from stableboys to the doctor who examined her, how she lay before him with her knees spread and cast off the sheet and brought his face to her breasts, held him with her legs, and how she wrenched him from his work and wife and child just for the challenge of it. That's all he was, poor bastard—a challenge. I wasn't even a challenge. I had money and I laid it at her feet, kissed her feet, begging her to love me. But she didn't love me. She drove me mad with desire and jealousy, telling me about the men she'd had—how they loved her for her breasts alone. I did. I knew the first time

I put my lips to those breasts that I would have to have her forever and always and I did not care what stood between me and Charlotte's body." He sputtered with liquor and derision, "I haven't entered her bedroom or her body for years. How many years?"

"What about the doctor, Austin?" I asked, as afraid of the question as the answer.

He wound his fingers around the neck of the bottle and brought it to his lips. "Dead."

"Yes, but—"

"He was alive once, wasn't he? Alive when he walked into the bedroom and found me lying naked on top of his wife. Oh, will God ever forgive me? Will I burn in hell for my sins?"

"What did Charlotte do—when he walked in?"

"Charlotte? Charlotte the harlot? She pushed me off and told him to come in and close the door. She got out of bed and raised her arms to heaven, and her breasts were as two young roes! And she laughed and said—am I the woman caught in adultery, Bill? She walked to the fire and we could both see the blue veins in her white thighs, and she said— can you cast the first stone, Bill? She leaned, naked against the marble mantelpiece, whose blue veins were so like her own, and she said, Charlotte said—do unto others, Bill, and you've done a little adultery unto others, haven't you, Bill? Now it's being done unto you. And Dabney, I was ashamed. I pulled the sheet over my body and Charlotte said, don't bother, Austin, the Doctor is well acquainted with the human body. The Doctor raised his fist to her. I thought he would knock her across the room, but she wasn't even frightened. You couldn't see a bit of fear in her eyes. She was spectacular."

In the heat cast by the fire, the red veins on Austin's nose pulsated, his lips and chins sagged and glowed with perspiration. For all the alcohol that warped his mind, Austin had kept Charlotte's distant body unblurred, as perfect as he once perceived it, but the effort cost him and he took a few more swigs and wiped his mouth with the back of his hand.

"What did the Doctor do then?" I asked.

"He slit his wrists. By nightfall he was dead. Went into the bathroom, rolled up his sleeves, and used his own scalpel. Covered the floor with blood, that's what he did. But did I care? Did I care that I'd driven a man to his last mortal sin? I made love to his wife on the floor in the library beside his very coffin, that's what I did. After the funeral I came back here with his widow and I took off her black dress, button by button, yard of crepe by yard of crepe. Oh! The prince's daughter!" He held his bottle aloft. "This holds no brew equal to the prince's daughter—'thy navel is like a goblet which wanteth not liquor.' " He studied the bottle curiously. "You know, Dabney, when this runs out, Charlotte says she won't get me any more. She says it's Prohibition and I'll just have to do without."

"She just says that to be mean."

"I can't do without it. It's all I have. It's all that's between me and damnation. Yea, though I have repented and confessed my sins to the Lord, I shall burn in hell forevermore." He took the poker and prodded the fire, peering into it, seemingly for a better look at his own fate. "I'll go to hell, but I won't be alone. Charlotte's lovers will be there. Legions of them. Because what Charlotte knew about the body she didn't learn from anatomy books. *I learned mine from an artist, Austin!* She told me so. She liked to tell me. She liked to drive me mad with jealousy and desire. And now her lovers drive me mad with jealousy and desire. They torment me, the dead ones. Now I'm afraid of Favour. I'm really afraid, Dabney. I keep waiting for him."

"Favour?"

"Afraid of his spirit. It will come to torment me like all the others. Lots of spirits come to me. They tell me things, but I never know who they are. I'd recognize Favour, though, just like I recognized the Doctor. Oh, I never mistook him. He came to me in the hospital, when they had swaddled me up tight like the baby Jesus and I couldn't move and they wouldn't let me out. I was a prisoner there and they didn't believe me about the Doctor—take him away, I begged them all, and they said I was crazy and gave me drugs, but it was the Doctor, whom I helped kill, who poured lye on my tongue—burning burning till I promised to make it all straight with him. I promised I'd never sleep with his wife again and he laughed and laughed all over my cell, for days I heard him laughing, because"—Austin took a deep drink—"even he knew she didn't want me by then."

"You were sick, Austin, and they just made you sicker."

"You won't tell about the Doctor, will you? If Charlotte knew he was here, his spirit even"—Austin looked furtively about. "He's watched them, Duckworth and Charlotte and whoever else. I've watched them. Oh, I have." Austin began to sniffle. "Charlotte made me."

"She made you?" I felt sick. I hoped that this was only an alcoholic delusion.

"Well, Duckworth. I called him scum and he told me what he was going to do to my wife and he—he's slime! Dirt! Filth!" Austin spluttered. "Naked and he came up to me and he said the Duckworths were great when the Courtneys and the Fairchilds were still"—he lost his train of thought and looked for it in the bottle.

"When the Fairchilds were still grubbing roots?" I asked, remembering the phrase from that horrible morning with Eugene. I began to wonder about his Lost Plantation Story. I had made light of it, of course, but might it mean more to him—a good deal more—than I had guessed?

"Yes. Grubbing roots. That's what he said. I said *impossible!* He has no honor, Dabney. None. No honor and I would not let him defile my wife." Austin began to cry openly.

"If it's too painful, Austin, you don't need to go on."

"It's always painful, Dabney. It doesn't matter if you talk about it or not. It's painful just the same." He took another quick swill from the bottle. "I told them: the Doctor watches you. Just as he watched me and Charlotte in life that day he came in and found us, he watches in death too. They never believed me. I told them how he tormented me in the hospital. I'd already repented my sins, begged God's forgiveness, and the repentance would have been enough for God, but the dead—the dead—" Austin's pale eyes searched over me, as if to make certain I was amongst the living. His hand came up and gently touched my hair.

"What about the dead, Austin?"

"The dead are more demanding. He wanted something else from me and even when they brought me back to Belle Haven, he didn't leave me, tormented me, sleeping and waking, but I never dared call out his name for fear they'd put me back in the hospital. Night after night, day after day I said to him—what do you want? What shall I seek? What shall I find and whither? Whither? He led me all over Belle Haven. The house, the grounds, and he tormented me for— for I don't know how long. Time lost its shape."

"What did he want?"

"I don't know. I never found it." He finished off the bottle. "I need another drink."

"I think you need some rest." I helped him stand and he took my hand and I led him to his room, though he stopped off first in one of the bathrooms, went straight to the commode and stood on a stool and reached into the high toilet tank and pulled out a fresh bottle of whiskey.

"Get some sleep, Austin," I said, settling him on the couch in his room. "You'll feel better."

"I'll never feel any better. Only Jesus can redeem me. God help me, I loved her. I did."

"God will understand," I said, speaking impetuously for the Almighty.

"And what about Favour? You think he'll torment me too?"

"Favour's torment is over."

"But suicides never rest. Their spirits roam the earth forever. They stay chained to the earth, to the living. They stay chained to the people who drove them to it. I'm afraid of Favour, even though I know he was brought here to poison me—Duckworth brought him here to kill me."

"Favour couldn't have poisoned anyone. He didn't have the brains."

"He didn't need them. Charlotte has them. That's enough. She'll find someone else to murder me and then she'll inherit all my money."

"Charlotte doesn't need to murder you to control your money, Austin." Even I knew that Austin hadn't controlled his own money in years. "Forget Favour, he's gone."

"Gone? Of course he's not gone! He died at Belle Haven, didn't he? None of the dead leave Belle Haven. Not even the living escape this place. Except you. You must escape." He clutched my wrist forcibly. "You're young, Dabney, and you must escape because the dead are just waiting for their day, you know, they're waiting down at the boathouse for the day when they will bring Belle Haven down, smite it like God smote Soddom and Gomorrah. They'll stop at nothing."

"The boathouse?" I said with a curious lump in my throat. "The boathouse?"

He brought his fierce, hot breath to my cheek. "The dead live there—Favour and the Doctor, they're there. They're waiting."

"Why there?"

"That's where he left me. I know he's there."

"Who?"

"The Doctor, Dabney. I told you the Doctor led me all over Belle Haven and that's where he wanted to be. To rest. He never tormented me again after I took him to the boat-house. Or he took me. Do you think that was it? Did he take me? That's why no one goes there anymore. The dead live there. The Doctor and Favour are there. They're waiting for their chance to kill Charlotte. I know it. I told the Doctor— I said, I repented, but Charlotte will never repent of what she did to you. You can never torment Charlotte. You'll have to kill her. And they will. Isn't it wonderful, Dabney? He never came back for me after I left him in the boathouse, so I know that's where he is." Austin suppressed a chuckle and lay down and I brought a quilt from the bed to cover his massive shivering frame and left him.

I went back to my room and stared at the rain sluicing down the windows and the dim, gray-gold world outside, everything rendered indistinct as a watercolor left in the rain. It came to me at that moment with unleavened clarity: the dead had not only spoken to Austin Courtney, but through him as well. I knew what Bay Hamilton wanted and I knew where it was.

13

I stamped my feet in the bitter cold of dawn. Belle Haven Lake looked much as it had before Favour was found floating in it—no telltale banner of blood marred its surface—but November was not kind and the water had a bronze sheen. The surrounding hills had lost their fiery splendor and dead leaves covered the ground like the coat of a shaggy camel. Bare branches rattled in the wind; the red and gold of October had died and the land lay gray as long-dead coal.

The three little boats were tied at the dock, the *Charlotte* still spattered with blood, which had dried to the color of powdered rouge. The vines and undergrowth that threatened to engulf the boathouse had lost their lush green mantle and appeared as sinewy, aged claws clinging to that doomed structure. As I waited at the door for Bay and reconsidered my conversation with Austin in the cold light of dawn, I felt very much the fool. Crazy even to be there.

Lots of spirits talked to Austin, I didn't doubt that; spirits very often reside in bottles of spirits, but that I should have taken his word as the truth, even indicative of the truth, seemed utterly irresponsible to me now. And I wondered if perhaps I believed Austin for no other reason save that I wanted to see Bay Hamilton again. One can always find reasons for doing what one wants and knows one shouldn't. One can always picket desire with the neat fence of necessity. At least, I chided myself, I should have waited and given my intuition the test of a few hours' time before I went to the phone in the library and asked the operator to connect me with Dr. Hamilton. A woman answered the phone, a woman with a sweet, tentative voice. I knew it was his mother. She said he was with a patient and could she take a message. I was just about to hang up when she said he'd finished and would be there in a minute.

I still could have hung up. I almost did.

"Dr. Hamilton," he said, as if it were a title instead of a simple name.

"This is Dabney Beale of Belle Haven," I announced emphatically, "and I don't want you to say anything, just listen to me." (I could almost hear the adenoidal breath of the operator, listening in; they did it all the time.) "I have what you want. Meet me at the usual place at the usual time." Then I hung up. And then I opened the decanter and had a quick swig of brandy. Prohibition be damned.

As I waited at the lake for Bay, I wished I hadn't chosen a November dawn. The barest rim of light showed over the hill, like a crack in the earth's cover; perhaps Bay wouldn't even come. Perhaps I would have to do this by myself, because I knew I could not rest until I knew for certain whether Austin was right and the dead did live on here. I was about to open the door alone when I heard Bay's horse crashing through the underbrush. I stood my ground, pulled myself to my full height, chin lifted, hands clenched, prepared to meet my enemy, my lover.

Bay tied his horse loosely to a tree and walked towards me. His pants were tucked into his riding boots and his shirt was open at the collar despite the early chill. He gave no word of greeting, did not speak till we were face to face. "Well, Dabney, what's all this about?"

"I might ask you the same question, Dr. Hamilton, if I had time to listen to your lame excuses."

"I never lied to you, Dabney."

"You never told me the truth, either."

"Did you call me here to match wits?"

"Far be it for me to match your wits, Bay Hamilton. You save your wit-matching for Charlotte; she's your equal, not me."

He colored angrily. "It was impossible for us from the beginning, Dabney. I never should have let it go as far as it did. I never should have allowed myself to fall in love with you."

"Spare me the romantic theatricals. Save them for Marjorie Vail. I'm sure she enjoys them."

"I told you I was going to Judge Vail. Marjorie just happened—"

"Please, I don't want to hear it."

"Anyway, I'm leaving this area as soon as I'm free to do so."

"Free of your sainted, suffering mother?" Were those not Charlotte's exact words, her inflection? I hastened on, hoping that Bay would not notice that bitterness and defeat were turning me into a pale version of the aunt I detested, and in that same cold, imperious tone, I added, "Your father's things are in the boathouse."

"What makes you think that?"

"Austin said so—more or less."

"Austin? Austin Courtney is a hopeless drunk."

"Yes, but—" I hated to continue, but I did and as I spoke to this perfectly sober man, Austin's drunken delusions sounded all the more ludicrous. I thought Bay might actually break out laughing, but he didn't.

"He said my father's spirit came to him and led him here?" Bay repeated carefully after me, as if I were a patient whose symptoms needed clarification.

"I admit Austin's not the most reliable person, but there was something about his voice . . . I believed him."

"You believe he has conversations with the dead?"

"Maybe. Maybe it was just guilt."

"Guilt?"

"Austin feels horribly guilty. The day he died, your father found Austin and Charlotte and they were—" I could not go on.

"Never mind, we're here. Shall we have a look?"

The boathouse door opened easily, and slowly my eyes adjusted to the pale gloom. We stood in the small room facing the three doors that led to the changing cubicles, which had not been used or explored in years. The only light filtered through the missing boards in the roof, where a part of the ceiling had caved in. Rats scuffled at our approach and spiders wound themselves more tightly into their webs. Puddles of standing water supported the life of those bugs that had survived the autumn's frost; beneath our feet the very floor seemed mushy, swollen, waterlogged, as if the lake had invaded the boathouse's very foundation. On the walls hung life rings with *Alicia, Francesca,* and *Charlotte* printed across them. The sheriff's men had rewound the lines neatly, and the three sets of oars were back on the walls. It all smelled of mold, mildew, and rot.

The boathouse had never been equipped with electricity and Bay asked me if there was a lamp. I thought I'd once seen one in the cabinet above the oars, but since Favour's death everything had been relocked and bolted. Bay fingered the heart-shaped lock on the cabinet and muttered something about ridiculous affectations and then he put his gloved fist through the cabinet door as if it were a wall of cotton candy. He seemed to enjoy it. He returned with the lantern and I could hear oil sloshing in the base. Kneeling, he lifted the globe and struck match after match, cursing until the thing took light. He brought it up to my face and it glowed feebly between us.

Bay's skin was still smooth and supple, but his eyes looked older, deeper set, as if they had retreated into his head. His thick hair, I noticed for the first time, was marred by a visible sprinkling of gray. His mouth, though grimly set, still looked lush and inviting and I dared not stare at it too long. "Where should we begin?" I asked.

"Perhaps you should have asked Austin."

We inspected the changing cubicles one by one; they yielded nothing but wicker chairs, gnawed and rotted beyond repair, and a few moldy cushions, bits of clothing, a random shoe—nothing more. Nor did any of the other cabinets have anything of interest save for the leftover paint with which I'd so carefully refurbished the boats last spring—now a million years ago. We did not speak until we'd searched every cabinet, crevice, and cranny, and then Bay once again held the lantern to my face, as if he wished to inspect my eyes for dementia. "Well, Dabney, you called me on a fool's errand and I came. What shall we do now?"

"Do whatever you damn please," I retorted.

"Shall I?"

He put his arm around my shoulders and drew me against his chest. His lips met mine in a kiss that was not the tender caress of last summer's gentle lover—not this time. He forced my mouth open for his searching tongue and though my heart constricted, my body's every filament quivered. I felt weak, as if my bones were made of wax melting over the flame. I pushed him away. "Don't you ever touch me again."

"You needn't worry. That was goodbye. You and I can never see each other again. We can never have anything more than what we've had."

"What we've had!" I nearly screamed. "What *you* had. You wanted revenge on Belle Haven and you got it."

"No, Dabney—Belle Haven has had its revenge on me. That's what happened. With that one wilful act, the seduction of my father, Charlotte Fairchild tainted three lives. Whatever happened to my parents, I ought to have been able to live beyond that act. I might have. I would have, had I not met you, fallen in love with you. I would have done my best to get my father's papers back and gone on with the rest of my life. I would have done my work, country doctor, helping people in and out of this world, setting their bones." Bay spoke almost wistfully. "But from that first morning when I met you at this lake, I felt so—so connected to you, such profound attachment and desire and—well, you know all that."

"So you've said," I retorted.

"I should have had the strength after that first morning never to return, but I could not deny what I felt for you and I kept coming back because I knew you would come too. And every time I left, every day that passed, I vowed, *This is the last, this is the last, but let me have just this one more day with her.*"

"Liar," I said with less conviction than I might have wished.

"You touched my heart and my soul and my body, Dabney. And I touched yours." He paused, as though he expected me to agree, but I remained silent. "But the taint from Belle Haven is so deep that it reaches even here, at this magical lake. That taint would follow us wherever we went. It followed your mother and father to London and back. It drove your father to suicide five years ago. It drove my father to suicide and my mother to a kind of living death and it wouldn't be any better or different for us. Because it's not just Charlotte. I don't know what it is, but it's something else. She has absorbed and reflects it. We've absorbed it too."

"Speak for yourself," I snapped.

"You sound just like her. Often. You know you do."

If I had opened my mouth I would have proved him irrefutably correct.

"I torment myself wondering if we could have gone about it any other way, if we would have felt the same passion had we not met at this lake, had we met at some white-gloved tea, some socially acceptable cotillion. I wonder if our lives would have been different, easier, if we'd sipped punch at a tea dance where young men say polite things to young ladies."

The thought made my skin crawl. "Young ladies like that simpering twit, Marjorie Vail?"

"I suppose. Her or someone like her."

Unreasoning rage rose in my breast, consuming, furious and implacable rage at the very idea of young men and young ladies and Marjorie Vail and Merrywell College and a man who wanted to tread in all those well-known rutted paths. I needed somehow to live up to reckless, wanton, wicked Belle Haven, to this passionate place, and I didn't give a damn what it cost me. I quickly unbuttoned my skirt, and it fell to the floor, and I shed my jacket before my skirt even pooled about my feet. I pulled the buttons off my blouse and flung it off, stepped quickly out of my knickers and stockings and yanked at the camisole ribbons impatiently, gave up, tugged at the straps till they tore. It fell from my shoulders. My breasts were bare, my nipples taut with cold, and I was naked. "Does Marjorie Vail come to you like this, Bay?"

He regarded me silently, as though he fought all the words that might have sprung to his lips. He put the lantern on the floor and for a moment I thought that he was going to kneel before me, his lips between my breasts, that he would strip off his gloves and feel me as I longed to feel him, but he did not touch me. "If I take your virginity, you'll hate me even more than if I don't."

"Then what have you got to lose?" I said in a brittle, nasty manner. "You might as well. Unless of course you want to keep yourself pure for the Marjorie Vails of this world."

He took off his gloves. "I love you more than heaven and earth and I would give heaven and earth to take you now, to take your virginity, to make love to you, but I won't because I can't do anything else. I can't marry you. I can't take you away from here. I can't even go on loving you the way a man loves a woman. I told you this was goodbye. I have not betrayed you, Dabney. Belle Haven has betrayed us both." He picked my skirt up off the floor, raised it to my hips, and fastened it at my waist, although his fingers trembled. He picked up my camisole and blouse, but they were ripped and hopelessly tattered. He gathered up my jacket and slid it over my arms. I could hear his breath coming, short and fast, while I listened to my buttons snap with a nearly audible finality. I flung my head back and let the tears stream down my face as I watched the lantern's wavering beams play over the ceiling. The light flickered over the peeling paint and splintered wood and I closed my eyes against the weeping that threatened to engulf me. When I opened my eyes again the ceiling contours appeared to have altered and a foursquare pattern emerged out of the wood, almost indistinguishable from the rest of the ceiling; it appeared, vanished, reappeared as the lantern light played over it. "What's that?" I said.

"What's what?" Bay had finished with the last button on my jacket and stepped away from me.

"Up there. The ceiling."

I held the lantern as Bay found a chair whose cane bottom had long since disintegrated, but he brought it over and balanced his feet on the frame, pushing against the edges of the foursquare pattern in the ceiling. It was clearly loose, but it didn't give way. Bay jumped down from the chair, grabbed an oar, and hammered at each of the four corners and the center. Flakes of paint drizzled over us, and finally with a rather muffled, soggy thump the square moved a bit. Bay hit it again forcibly with the oar, once, twice, and on the third try it came loose and fell, nearly hitting Bay on its way to the floor, where it crashed, filling the air with dust and splinters. Above us we could see a half-lit void.

"Stand by the door, Dabney—if the boards are rotten, I don't want to fall on you." Bay hoisted himself up. The ceiling sagged beneath his weight, but did not give way.

"What do you see?"

"It's too dark. Can you pass the lantern up?"

I looped the lantern handle over an oar and, standing on the chair, I hoisted it through the narrow opening. Bay took it, set it aside, and then lay on his stomach and extended his hands to me. "Take hold of my arms and jump, and I'll pull you up."

I thought surely the beams would give way with both of us up there, but they did not and I found myself in a tiny unfinished air space between the roof and ceiling. We had to crawl on all fours, but against the wall we could just make out neat stacks of books. Medical books, that much was clear as Bay brought the lantern closer. He took one of the books, its pages stuck together, its rim furred with green mold. On the flyleaf in an old-fashioned Spencerian hand was written: *William B. Hamilton, M.D.*

"So," Bay said grimly, "Austin was right."

I stayed where I was, afraid we'd upset the balance of nature in this grim crawlway, worried that bats might swoop overhead or spiders attack me, but the scuffling all seemed to come from the woodwork where Bay was digging. He brought back the lantern and a black bag, a physician's bag. He pried it open.

Inside were a dozen small notebooks, each with MEDICAL RECORDS stamped in gold on them. The early ones, from the 1890s, were crammed full of daily entries—patients' names, descriptions of their symptoms, and the medicines prescribed and prognosis, sometimes including a sensitive observation on the patient's state of mind, or a philosophical note that suggested a scholarly man in the midst of a busy life. The latter ones, those from the years after Dr. Hamilton had become entwined with Belle Haven, were sparse, with weeks passing between laconic entries.

"He didn't practice much at the end, I guess."

"How could he? My father could hardly expect his patients to come to Belle Haven. He could hardly return to Oakstone to practice in the surgery that was part of our house. My mother kept that office immaculate, just as if she always expected him back."

"Or expected you to use it one day."

"Yes, she probably expected that, too. My mother never raises her voice above a whisper and still gets everything she wants."

"Almost everything," I corrected him. "She wanted your father back and she didn't get him."

"Some things are irrevocable." He shuffled through the notebooks till he came to the one marked 1900, and he flipped through the pages with the determined air of a man who knows exactly what he is looking for and dreads finding it. "Here it is," he said at last. "I've often wondered."

"What?"

Bay passed me the book and I read: *November 1—Charlotte Fairchild. Age 22. Treated for miscarriage, more likely induced (self-induced?) and badly botched abortion. Fever. Bleeding. Extent of internal damage not yet known.*

Bay found other entries, numerous entries for when Dr. Hamilton had seen Charlotte professionally, when she had returned to his office time and again. In one of his notations (which became increasingly terse and laconic) he noted she would never bear children as the result of this "incident." The word was his.

"So that's how it happened," Bay said without rancor. "That's why she came to him and that's how it happened. I had often wondered."

I remembered what Austin had told me, could imagine how pleased Charlotte must have been to have seduced the doctor in his own office, the one attached to his house, with his wife and son, so to speak, in the very next room. But I remained silent as Bay dug down to the bottom of the cracked leather bag and drew forth two envelopes, both with their seals broken, both addressed in the elder Dr. Hamilton's unmistakable hand—one addressed to Charlotte and one addressed to Mrs. Margaret Hamilton, Oakstone, Virginia. The latter had a stamp on it. Bay held them in either hand, as if he were weighing them in the balance. "One liar always recognizes another," he said cryptically.

"Your father?"

"No. Charlotte. Charlotte knew I was lying."

"Lying about what?"

"Charlotte was right—all I wanted to do was make the gallant effort. Isn't that what she called it? She knew that I never truly wanted to find this at all." He crumpled the two envelopes in his fists.

"Maybe you didn't know it until just now."

"What good can this letter do? It will only resurrect all that pain. My mother is suffering with enough physical pain, she doesn't need all this old, remembered suffering brought to life. She thinks she hasn't forgotten it, but she has. One must. One does. Our minds are kinder to us than we know. But when she reads this, all that pain will rip across her heart again and this time it will be my fault."

"You don't have to give them to her."

"No. What's one more lie, after all? It's only—I cringe to think how clearly Charlotte Courtney saw what I was about."

"Then why did you come here today if you didn't truly want them?"

"For you. I came to see you."

"What's one more lie?" I shrugged and shoved the medical journals back into the bag.

"Yes," he replied tersely, "what's one more?" He opened the letter addressed to Charlotte: a single page of cream-colored Belle Haven stationery embossed with the usual insignia—BH entwined in a heart. He read it silently and handed it to me as if it were a wood chip. "There are no surprises here. It's exactly what you'd expect a man who was married to Charlotte to write just before he killed himself."

I curse the day I met you. From the first I have put aside my ethics for you. My medical ethics, my duties to my wife and son, finally, now, even my responsibilities to myself and God. But I cannot leave this life without telling you that I know you for what you are. You used my skills to repair the only miscalculation you ever made in your life. You used my heart to revenge yourself on your sister Julia. You've used my body and my soul. My mind is all I have left and I will die before I will let you corrupt that as well.

Don't think for a moment that this is the result of finding you in bed with Courtney. Courtney is a fool. Not the first fool. Not the last.

I'll see you in hell.

I folded the letter along its previous lines and slid it back into the envelope. Bay handed me the second one, having already read it. This time he said nothing.

My darling Margaret—
I don't write this to ask your forgiveness. I've gone beyond forgiveness and I know that your pride would never allow you to bestow that forgiveness much as your heart might beg of you to do so. I don't even ask for your

understanding because I know that what I did must seem forever incomprehensible to you. It remains incomprehensible to me. Perhaps passion always remains outside the realm of rationality and can never be understood except at the moment it's being committed, the very moment when one is least able to understand anything at all.

Nothing in your gentle nature, my darling wife, would permit you to comprehend what I have gone through, what I have brought myself to, what I have sunk to, or allow you to understand such destruction as I've encountered in the woman I left you for.

Darling Margaret, I beg of you only that you not let our son grow up to hate his father, that you spare me some tiny shard of your pity and understanding and compassion, that you think of me as sick, if need be, but not evil. What I am about to do, my darling Margaret, is but the logical outcome of my having abandoned you, my profession, my son, and all that I was taught is useful or necessary to the conduct of life. Even now your purity stands before me as a beacon and a reproach.

My dearest love to you and Billy.

William

"Billy?" I said.

"That was me."

He put both letters in his pocket and turned away. I wanted to touch him, to offer some morsel of comfort or hope, the old human effort to soothe the unsoothable, to offer balm to pain and ease to suffering, but when one most needs them, such efforts are utterly without value or efficacy. "Will you show your mother the letter?"

"I don't know."

"Maybe you could tell her you found the books, but not the note."

"A half lie."

"A half truth."

He turned back to the books and pulled a few out. The orderly stacks tottered and fell; as they tumbled all around us, we coughed in the blizzard of dust and flying mold. Bay cursed as he began restacking them.

"I don't see any reason to do that," I said. "I mean, whoever stacked them there in the first place isn't likely to come back."

"And who might that be?"

I didn't know. I guessed Charlotte, but couldn't imagine her here on all fours patiently stacking a bunch of medical books when she might just as easily have tossed them out. I was about to venture this guess when behind the fallen books something caught my eye, and I stayed Bay's arm. "What's that? There, behind the books, shoved up against the wall. What's that?"

The lantern dimmed, flickered, and went out, but the morning sun fell through the holes in the roof, and as Bay pulled away the last few books several long cylinders rolled out. They stopped against my knee. They looked like bolts of heavy cloth tied with thick, black grosgrain ribbon.

Bent double, like peasants carrying heavy sheaves, we toted them toward the thin sunshine now spilling through the broken half of the roof. I tugged at the ribbons, but the knots were stubborn. Bay took out a small pocket knife and released the fabric with one swift surgical movement. He held the edges, and as I unrolled it I could hear the canvas crackling gently with a sound I recalled from my dimmest childhood: paint crackling on canvas.

A dark background of indigo blue paled to a pearly hue and thence to a silvery gray, richly textured, patterned almost, like wallpaper or fabric. Indeed, it was fabric and painted across it lay a recumbent, nude female figure, the apricot tints of her skin in brilliant contrast to the ashen satin everywhere around her, the sort of contrast one sees when one places a lighted candle beside a frost-covered pane—Charlotte, with her head thrown back and her long hair lost in the folds of satin; Charlotte, her mouth open and the tips of her white teeth visible. *Charlotte.* With one hand spread between her ripe breasts she seemed to be taking pleasure or maybe simple comfort from the beat of her own heart. *Charlotte.* Signed *A.D.B. 1899.* Oh yes, the body was Charlotte's, but the eyes were the eyes of the fox in the dining-room mural. Eyes A.D.B. knew well. How well? Carnally. *Charlotte.* Her other hand was casually outflung and her fingers were tensed around a blue-black plum. I almost expected to see the plum burst beneath the grip of those fingers and its juices stain the rest of the painting, which included other fruit—grapes and over-ripe pears and mottled apples. Charlotte's pink, perfect toes seemed to rest against an overturned silver dish, which apparently had once held the scattered fruit. Corrupt fruit from corrupt trees.

"Decadent," said Bay, "but effective."

He broke the ribbon on the second one, signed *A.D.B.* and dated 1901. This nude was upright, equally voluptuous: *the prince's daughter. The joints of thy thighs are like jewels. Thy belly is like a heap of wheat set about with lilies . . . thy breasts are as clusters of grapes.* Her belly was indeed the delicate color of wheat, and tendrils of pubic hair graceful as lilies sprouted between her thighs. Her mouth was curled with knowledge and satisfaction.

"What is it, Dabney?" asked Bay. "Surely you can't be shocked she'd pose nude, knowing what you do of her."

"My father," I said stonily. "A.D.B., my father." And if Austin were right and the legions of Charlotte's dead lovers met in hell, my father would be there. Was my father amongst Austin's many spirits? Austin would not have recognized him. But Charlotte would when she met him in hell. And to think of the hell she created. Had she chronicled my father's intimacies to Austin as well? Tormented Austin with my father?

What had she learned of anatomy from the artist? What indeed? "My father was her lover too. The child she aborted would have been my brother. My cousin and my brother."

Bay reached out his hand to me, but I could not take it. I could not move. "Maybe your parents weren't married when those were painted," Bay offered.

"Oh, don't be so legalistic! What does that matter? Look at her face! My father betrayed my mother just like your father betrayed your mother. For Charlotte!"

"You can't undo it," he said at last. "Your father is dead."

"So is yours," I retorted.

"I've had years to absorb my bitterness, but yours is so fresh, so—"

"But you haven't absorbed it, Bay. Please don't try to tell me that you have. If you had, you would have loved me just now, the way I wanted. You would have made love to me last summer the way I wanted. The way *you* wanted too, but for—for all this rot from the past! So please don't tell me how you've tidied everything up and gone about your own life."

"I'd like to." The pain in his face touched me. "I'd like to go on with my life with you, Dabney."

"But that's impossible. You said so yourself." I wanted him to contradict me, to tell me that it wasn't so, that we could flee Belle Haven forever, that the shock and revulsion I felt could be denied. With a pang of combined weariness and revulsion I was unwillingly reminded of that morning episode with Eugene—when he had said that the past dominates and motivates all human intercourse. *I use the word advisedly.* I wanted to retch. I almost did. "I hate the past and everything connected with it. Charlotte. My father. Belle Haven. Even you," I added bitterly.

"That's not true. You don't hate me. You love me. I won't let you think or say anything different. You love me and I love you."

"Is that why you were prepared to leave me? You told me this was goodbye. Again."

"I thought it was for your own good. For my own good, but finding all the leftovers of other people's lives, I'm convinced."

"Convinced of what?"

"Don't you see, Dabney—I do, I understand it at last—if we part now, if we fail to love each other, then Charlotte Courtney's triumph will be complete. She'll be victorious over all of us. The living and the dead. We're the only ones who can defeat her, and we can do that only if we love each other."

I brought my hand to his bearded cheek and loved him at that moment the way an old woman might love her aged husband, not for his beauty and the strength of his limbs and the hot passion he once ignited in her, but for his understanding, his unquenchable kindness, his enduring loyalty, his unflagging generosity of spirit. And it was in this vein—not prompted by the lust that had so consumed me in the summer—but in this rich autumnal love that I put my arms around his neck and our clothes fell from our bodies like the leaves from the trees and we lay together naked and I gave my virginity and I took his love. As the chill November sun shed its pale light upon us through the broken roof, we warmed each other and I opened my mouth and my body and my heart all at the same splendid moment. We dignified, or perhaps enchanted, that sad old boathouse with our irrevocable love.

14

By the time I returned to Belle Haven the long shadows of
the short afternoon had already reached out across the boxwood maze and the smell of smoke from the evening's fires
blew towards me. I would have entered the house through
the dining room, which was the easiest route, but I had no
wish to see the eyes of that fox again. So I went through the
spare, denuded patio and let myself into the main hall, and
as I closed the door behind me Charlotte stepped out of the
library.

"God almighty! Where have you been? You look awful."

I glanced in the hall mirror and was taken aback at my own
reflection. I had not bothered to put my hair back up and it
lay loosely around my shoulders, with leaves and flecks of
paint caught in it. My face was streaked with dust and my
clothes were rumpled and dirty. Mercifully I had put my
stockings back on, but my blouse with its broken buttons and
my torn underwear were crumpled up underneath my buttoned jacket. I clutched all this tightly. This and one other
thing, because as the sunlight had shifted over Bay and me
that day, it had eventually illuminated the darkest corner of

those rafters, and in the very back Bay and I spied a shallow keyless box with a dull heart-shaped lock. We fought with the lock, but it was stubborn; Bay said that meant it was not to be opened and I should throw it in the lake and be done with the past. I was tempted. The present was so glorious I was tempted, but Bay had also given me the courage to face the past.

But at that moment in the front hall Charlotte had caught me quite off guard and I was cowed and startled.

"Well, answer me. Where have you been, looking like that?"

"I fell." The lie burbled easily to my lips; in the biblical sense I was certainly telling the truth. "I have fallen," I said rather grandly, "down into the ravine."

"Well, you look as if you've fallen down the Himalayas. Come into the library. Eugene and I want to talk to you. We just got back a few hours ago and we've been looking everywhere for you."

"I'm really very tired, Charlotte."

"Come into the library, Dabney."

"Let me get changed first. I can't see Eugene looking like this." Indeed I knew I could not see Eugene or bear the sight of his smug, upturned lips. Eugene would know, and I might never have been safe again.

"I'm not presentable."

Charlotte by contrast was very presentable. Her hair seemed brighter—the color refurbished—and freshly cut, with the same bobbing curl that fell seductively against her cheek. She was dressed in a smart traveling suit of cinnamon-colored wool and she sported a fading corsage of spider mums on her lapel. Her silk blouse lay smoothly over her shoulders, but her bones protruded at the collar; she was no longer the well-fleshed ripening peach of the woman in the paintings, but desiccated and splintery.

"Well, what are you staring at? Get a move on and get back down here."

I refreshed myself quickly, washed my face, put on clean clothes, then brushed the leaves from my hair and knotted it at the back of my neck. I wrapped the rusted metal box in a nightgown and put it in the bottom drawer of the bureau. On my way downstairs I encountered Austin, who was drunk, clutching the balustrade with one hand and supporting the fresh bottle of whiskey, concealed beneath his coat, with the other.

He brought his fingers to his lips and his eyes rolled back in his head as if he were searching for his brains. "Shhh, Dabney, they're back, you know. Take care, Dabney. Take care. There's something different. Something wicked. More wicked. I can feel it."

I found Charlotte and Eugene sipping brandy in the library before a crackling fire that played over their faces, lighting the hollows in Eugene's cheeks, emphasizing the glitter in Charlotte's eyes. As I entered their voices fell to a hush and Charlotte suppressed a short laugh.

"Well, Dabney." Eugene gazed at me as if I were a piece of antique furniture he intended to bid on. "What have you been doing these past two weeks?"

"Nothing." I took a seat near the fire.

"You don't look as if you'd been doing nothing."

"Reading, then."

"Don't be dull, Dabney," said Charlotte, kicking off her shoes. "We've had a miserable journey down from New York and I'm not in the mood."

"You said you wanted to talk to me. What about?"

"Right to the point, aren't we? My, my, Dabney, have you got a burr under your bridle?"

"Bridles are for horses."

Charlotte rubbed her stocking feet together lazily. "I've

had a letter from Alicia. She'll be here in a few days, so it looks as if we'll have to decide what to do with you."

I set my lips firmly and watched the fire.

"Aren't you interested in what we're going to do with you, Dabney?"

"Will it matter if I am interested or not?"

"No, but I thought—"

"You thought you'd like to see me squirm and beg, didn't you? You've already told me I have no money, that I'm supposedly at your mercy."

"Supposedly!" Charlotte crowed.

"There's nothing you can do with me, Charlotte. I'm free."

"No one who is penniless is free, my dear."

"I can't be bullied anymore."

"Really, Dabney," Eugene remonstrated; he seemed tired, not his usual predatory self. "Who said anything about bullying? Your aunts are thinking of what's best for you."

"And what is best for me?"

"Alicia and I were thinking of marriage, Dabney dear."

"Marriage!"

"Yes, dear, here comes the bride. Marriage. The hallowed institution of love and honor and obedience."

"I don't want to get married."

"That's not the point."

"It's not to my advantage to marry."

"Quite the contrary. It is to everyone's advantage that you marry. It's what all the girls your age do, marry. You will become a respectable young matron and you can have the other young matrons in to tea and enjoy yourself to no end. Alicia and I will be shed of our burden and responsibility for your health and well-being, which will be assumed by your doting husband."

"And who might he be? Surely you have someone in mind."

"I do at that. You know, Dabney, Mr. Emery was quite smitten with you at the Belle Haven ball."

"He wasn't any such thing."

"Dabney underestimates her charms, doesn't she, Eugene? Mr. Emery asked me several times if he might call on you, but I thought you were too upset by poor Favour's death, but all that's past now and so I've invited Mr. Emery here tomorrow for lunch. And I expect you to be your sweet charming self, and if you're a very good girl, perhaps Mr. Emery will sweep you off your feet and kiss you in the garden."

My whole being revolted at the thought of clammy-handed, thin-lipped Mr. Emery. "Is this your idea of a joke?"

"Not at all. Alicia and I—"

"What does Alicia know of Mr. Emery?"

"Alicia will take my word for it. He is a nice young man, from a good family. Really, didn't they teach you anything at Merrywell? When I was there they very carefully instructed us to look for the three B's in a man. Bucks, Breeding, and Body."

"Aren't you forgetting brains?"

"Am I? Well, maybe so. Well, I can't speak for Mr. Emery's brains and his body isn't perhaps everything one might wish—at least to look at him clothed. When he's your husband of course that will be different. You might discover a whole new man beneath—"

"He'll never be my husband."

"But he certainly has breeding. The Emerys have been a famous family around these parts for a century."

"At least they didn't make their money in Grippit Glue," I said with a swift glance to Eugene.

Charlotte colored angrily. "Watch your tongue, you wretched little ingrate. In fact"—Charlotte toyed with her curl—"I was just coming to money. For all their breeding, the Emerys would be happy for a little infusion of money. And of course, I've indicated to Mr. Emery that my dear niece, my ward, would not come empty-handed. I would of course provide handsomely for any niece of mine who married into such an illustrious family as the Emerys."

"I'll never marry Mr. Emery. You can't make me. I'm not pregnant, you know."

"Well, who said anything about—that!" Charlotte exclaimed. "Really, Dabney, that's most uncouth. What kind of books have you been reading?"

"Anatomy books." I kept my gaze riveted to Charlotte's face. "I found some anatomy books and I've been reading them."

Shock decorated her face for half a second and Eugene got up and helped himself to more brandy. Charlotte tucked her feet underneath her like a cat. "Ring for the butler, Eugene, and have him bring another glass for Dabney."

"The butler?" My own shock was less well disguised.

"We have a new butler now."

Eugene rang and the three of us sat mutely, taking one another's measure in the lamplight. Presently there appeared a man who very nearly dwarfed the doorway. His massive chest and shoulders bulged from his butler's garb. He had black hair, and thick black brows met over his nose. He was clean shaven, though the black shadow of a beard was visible against his olive complexion. His eyes were smug and his lips thick and muscular-looking.

"Yes?" he said.

"Yes, madame," Charlotte corrected him.

"Yes, madame."

"We need another brandy glass for my niece. Oh, you two haven't met. This is my niece Dabney Beale. This is Anthony. Lovely name, don't you think, Dabney? It quite reminds me of your middle name."

"Yes." That's all I could reply. And barely that.

"Call me Tony," he said to me sullenly. "I don't like Anthony."

"But I do, I like Anthony very much. And you work for me now."

"Have it your way."

"You say 'Yes, madame.' "

"Yes, madame." He turned to leave.

"Will you stoke the fire please, Anthony?"

Effortlessly he lifted a huge log and tossed it into the fire. He squatted on his haunches to prod and poke at it, and his buttocks threatened to burst the seams of his pants. "Will that be all, madame?"

"I need a light." A cigarette perched perilously on Charlotte's lower lip. Anthony lit a taper and brought it to her, holding it just one quarter inch from the cigarette. Charlotte had to bend ever so slightly forward for her light. "That will be all. Except for the glass, of course. Ethel will show you which one to bring and you may tell her we'll dine in an hour's time."

He left us without speaking and Charlotte billowed blue smoke, smiling through it. "We found Anthony in New York. He came with very good references."

"I'm sure he did," I replied, my recent bravado shriveling inside me like burning blossoms; Anthony seemed to have drugged the very air we breathed with menace. He returned with the brandy glass.

"Now pour Dabney some and give it to her," Charlotte instructed him.

Anthony filled the glass half full and brought it to me, his eyes glowing with resentment.

"Thank you," I said weakly, "but I won't be needing it. I'm going to bed."

"Dis is good stuff," Anthony protested.

"You'd better take it with you, Dabney," Charlotte chimed in. "It will help you sleep—and you want to be sure to sleep well tonight."

I rose and stood beside Anthony. I came barely to the middle of his chest. I took the glass he offered me and made my way out of the library. As I crossed the hall I heard Charlotte break into razor-edged laughter. Eugene closed the library door as I heard him say, "I tell you, Charlotte, you underestimate that girl. She's not the little simpleton you think."

But Charlotte only laughed in response and told Anthony that that would be all. For now.

My teeth chattered as I took off my clothes, not so much from the cold but from the infectious ugliness Anthony exuded. I nearly screamed when a knock sounded at my door, but it was only Marian carrying a tray with some dinner and a pot of hot tea. Her eyes too were lit with fear and I knew now what Austin meant when he said something was different. "You've met the new butler, I guess."

Marian made an unmistakable gesture of spitting and then patted my head and left.

I put on a white flannel nightgown and wrapped a shawl around my shoulders before turning out the lights. I pulled my knees up to my chest and sat in the rocker by the dying fire, clutching the rusted metal box I'd found that afternoon. Austin's interminable prayers droned through the lathe and plaster. I added my prayers to his: Dear Lord—whatever happens in my aunt's bedroom tonight, don't let me hear it; don't let it touch me. Leave me what little innocence I have left.

But even as I prayed I knew I had no innocence left, not a single shred. It had nothing to do with the loss of my virginity—that seemed a trifle, a token. Indeed, I felt not at all like a fallen woman, but like a risen one—rising like the tide, like yeast, like the moon, like all the things Austin's God had placed in nature. No, my innocence was lost long before my virginity, lost before I was born, lost because of sins I did not commit and which I was about to discover.

15

The lock did not break easily. But I dug and twisted and pried, and finally the thing sprung open, the corroded hinges squealing as I opened the shallow box. Inside I found a handful of small sketches—geraniums, blades of grass, hands in various postures, feet, slender feet, breasts, small sketches of Charlotte nude. They were hurried and in some ways more interesting than the voluptuous model of the heavy painted canvases. They were of course the work of my father, the late and unlamented Anthony Beale, and it gave me great pleasure to feed them to the fire and watch them burn for all time. "Wilt thou take this woman?" I said to the fire and it did. It was the least I could do to Charlotte, who now wanted to inflict the final horror on me and marry me off to a man she knew I would hate.

Beneath the sketches, tied with rust-stained satin ribbon, were a few letters. The metal box had not been able to protect them from dampness and the envelopes were soggy, the ink swollen but the writing still distinguishable.

Miss Charlotte Fairchild
Belle Haven, Virginia.

The envelope had a British stamp and without so much as a pang of remorse or guilt, I pulled out the letter.

April 25, 1899

Darling darling,
Your father's letter came today and my answer is yes yes yes. I will write him to that effect later in a style more befitting the solemnity of his offer and compare him to the great English patrons of art who vanished a century ago and it will please him that I'm properly grateful. I shall not add that the prospect of painting without fear of the debt collector is not Belle Haven's chief attraction, but you, my little kumquat. You inspire me and you take me from my work. I can't decide if I should paint you or ravish you and were you not so beautiful, my work would go more quickly. The art world agrees with me that you are ravishingly beautiful, darling. *Woman with Geranium #1* (the one where you are nude in the window and the rim of your breast caresses the geranium) has just sold to Lady Ashwell, and no lesser personage than Lord Fleming has purchased *Woman with Geranium #3* for his private collection. I'd like to think that it was my art, but it was your lovely body, my little fig, my delicious little fig.

But darling—I have my doubts. It's easier to conceal a love affair in a city like London than in a place like Belle Haven. Shall I have to sit across the table from you and restrain myself from tearing your clothes from your body? Shall I have to make conversation with your wealthy papa and simpering sisters while I long to fill your navel with honey and lick it clean?

But I'll come of course. London is desolate without you and I find I can scarcely lift a brush without the assurance of your daily visit. Jimmy Whistler sends you his best and tells me I am a lucky man to have you as a model and a mistress. I hope he does not know the latter from experience.

My darling Charlotte I am your abject lover.

Anthony.

I burned it. There were a half dozen of the same ilk between that April date and June, when he arrived at Belle Haven. I burned them too, and it gave me enormous pleasure to burn letters that Charlotte had treasured, however many years it may have been since she had read them. Charlotte was shrewd and she would not have kept the letters or the paintings unless they'd meant a great deal to her. It was very unlike her to have kept them at all. But these, these lovesick, erotic messages told me only that my father had once loved my aunt. They did not so much as point to what happened next.

The letter was dated September 23, 1900, and postmarked Richmond, Virginia; it was written in the same hand, only far more hurriedly.

Charlotte—

Julia is sleeping and we have a train to catch in a few hours' time, but I must write. I know you and I know you will stop at nothing to tarnish my happiness with Julia, wreck and destroy it, but you must believe me, I never intended to fall in love with your sister and it happened both so slowly and so quickly I myself scarcely knew it.

In these last months I could not touch you, I could not look at you without longing for Julia. I told you the truth at last and you used that truth to blackmail me, to keep me coming to your bed or you would tell Julia of our affair. I am writing now to tell you that we are beyond your reach. We are going to England and we're going to be married and before we are, I shall tell Julia the whole truth myself so you needn't think that you can hurt us, or maim our love in any way. I love Julia in ways you can never understand, because you haven't a heart, Charlotte, much less a soul. Lies come easily to you and this nonsense about your being pregnant with my child is only one more lie, the last vengeance you have. You have always lied and used me brutally and I shall not be duped by you again.

Julia and I are going far away and we will never trouble you again. See that you return the favor.

Anthony Beale.

This one seemed to burn in my hand before I even tossed it towards the fire. *God pity the man Charlotte loves*—Eugene's flippant observation rang in my head. I could believe that my father was but one of many men who had loved Charlotte Fairchild, but was it possible, could it be, that he was the one man she had loved? Could Charlotte have so loved a man that she would blackmail him into her bed? The thought was almost preposterous. And yet. I could imagine, somehow, that when Charlotte had got Anthony Beale to her bed, how she must have clung to him, hung round his neck, threatened, cajoled, held on to his body as she could not hold on to his heart. Did he, when he came to Charlotte, did he still smell of Julia? Was Charlotte so very desperate that she deliberately courted social suicide in conceiving a child so that she could play on Anthony Beale's sense of honor and snatch him back from Julia? If indeed it had happened in this calculating way, she was very likely astonished that her lies had so sullied her credibility that he no longer believed her. If the pregnancy had been a simple error, then how horrified, how desolate she must have been to find herself pregnant by a man she despised socially, loved passionately, and could not have, because—quickly I snatched the letter from the fire and

looked again at the date: *September 23, 1900.* I was born in
April, 1901. Julia would already have been pregnant with me.
Of course Anthony would never have told Charlotte that,
never have given her that kind of ammunition. She might
have figured it out later, but she could not have known it
then.

So Anthony Beale had begotten children on both sisters,
eloped with Julia, and left Charlotte facing social destruction
(and even *I* could imagine how Charles Fairchild would have
greeted this news). Charlotte was pregnant, despairing, abandoned. Dr. Hamilton's records told the rest of the tale; Charlotte butchered herself to get rid of the child, then seduced
the only person who could have known her secret. And it
was a secret. Not the pregnancy and the abortion, but that
she had ever loved any man. Even Eugene did not know this
secret. A slight shudder went down my spine when I realized
it may have been the only secret he did not know.

I fed that to the fire and picked up the last letter in my
father's hand, which was almost indecipherable, as the writing
slanted in a slow, sad scrawl to the edge of the pages.

2 May 1904

Charlotte La Belle Dame Sans Merci,
Charlotte the Unforgetting
Charlotte the Unforgiving
Charlotte the Implacable—
Forgive me the unconventional salutation, but it's all that
words can do. If words could leap from this page and
wrap their talons round your throat and strangle the very
life out of you—I would bid them do so. But alas, you
were the one with the power to make words strangle
the life from me and I am left with this poor pen and
not the dagger you deserve. I should have known,
guessed—ah, remembered—that time was of no impor-

tance to you, that time would not mollify you, that neither time, nor age, nor experience would ease your heart, or your wrath. And the more fool I to have believed that I could simply leave Belle Haven and free myself, my wife, and my daughter from your malevolence. I should have known that neither time nor distance would stop you and I am well rebuked.

But was I so very evil? Did I deserve this fate? Did I deserve your wrath? I think not. I only did what every painter does who has a particularly beautiful and compliant model. I bedded you, but perhaps I did not even do that. Perhaps you bedded me. I cannot recall. You see—the experience was not so memorable after all. (I'm quite drunk now, but I think you bedded me, that's the way it was.) You were a society debutante and I painted your portrait like so many others and though I remember thinking how I would love to paint you in the nude, I don't remember suggesting it. In fact I think you first posed for me in the nude, lying on the narrow bed in my studio after, yes, after I had bedded you. Or you had bedded me. It was your idea and at the time I thought it was a lovely idea and you were a lovely woman, but having once bedded you, you infected me, got into my bloodstream like one of those nasty little parasites that gnaw out men's brains in the tropics, and I was sick with love for you.

Did I beg to return to America with you? No. What does that matter? I came, didn't I, allowed myself to be reduced to the level of a high-class servant at Belle Haven at the beck and call of your braggart father. And your beck and your call. Which was often. You were always insatiable.

And then there was Julia. Radiant Julia. I've been sitting here in the three days since Julia left me, drinking. I've drunk everything but the kerosene and I may start on that and for three days I have been asking, Julia, my love, my life, how could you leave me? But it's not Julia I should question, is it? I see that now. It's you. Finally I'm ready to ask the proper question: Why, Charlotte? Why did you wait four years? Why wasn't your letter here waiting for us when we arrived in London four years ago? Why didn't you tell her the very summer I fell in love with her, the very summer I was getting a leg up on you, Charlotte, as they say down at the pub, and taking less and less pleasure in it every time. And how did you know that I am such a coward that I would never tell Julia myself?

And on the third day, after Julia left me, this third day, I rose again and the answer came to me. Charlotte waited these four years, tensed her word-talons for four years, because she knew that if she'd told Julia in the beginning, it would not have mattered. Julia would have been hurt, but the buoyancy, the beauty, the energy of our love would have outlived the accusation. But four years—ah, four years of paint and poverty, four years of Julia sitting with her clothes off in drafty London tenements, four years of dwindling commissions, four years of watching one's own daughter go hungry. Four years in the dampest heart of gas-lit London—that would have undermined the love of angels, let alone us mere mortals. So you waited four years and then you wrote Julia and told her the truth. But—you lied just the same. You lied when you said I loved you. I never loved you. I loved the curve of your breast and the swell of your thighs and the colors in your curling short hairs, my dear, but I never loved you. I never loved any woman but Julia and she might even believe that, but she's left me just the same.

I salute you—Charlotte the victor, on a well-plotted campaign. You've vanquished me, conquered me, reduced my life to ash, reduced your sister's life to ash, and probably Dabney's life as well. All hail, Charlotte. All hail to you. I'm drunk, yes, but I write you this letter full of garlands, laurels. Rest on them while you can, because I'll meet you in hell.

I had never felt much of anything for my father, save for the hatred I conceived for him when I found those nude portraits of Charlotte that very morning. But as I read this letter, my hatred softened, jelled into compassion, and then my compassion dissolved into pity and I wept to think of his wasted life and squandered talent, his death noted only briefly, in a clipping from the London *Times* at the bottom of the box, which noted the demise of Anthony Dabney Beale in August of 1904. It said that Mr. Beale, a painter and friend of the late James McNeil Whistler, fell under the wheels of an incoming train at Victoria Station and that bystanders testified that he was drunk and disorderly at the time of his death. It said that Mr. Beale's only well-known works were a series of "modern classics" entitled *Woman with Geranium*.

That was it. Charlotte drove my father to what amounted to suicide and at the same time gave him his only bit of immortality.

Only one other letter lay in the bottom of the box, unbound and sticking out of its envelope. I recognized my mother's rather stiff, upright hand. I remembered her handwriting because, even when I was a child, it always reminded me of the way she walked: chin up, as though the weight of her hair could be balanced only by the excessive tilt of her head, shoulders squared, back straight. She never stooped, even for me. When she would put her arms around me, she knelt until we were the same height. I did not know what this letter held, but I could not believe that she had stooped for Charlotte, either.

December 18, 1904
New York

Charlotte—

I have just written to Father rejecting his offer that I
return to Belle Haven. I told him quite candidly that his
betrayal and desertion of me and my husband when we
most needed his love and understanding have forever
hardened my heart against the Fairchilds and Belle Haven and I prefer to live—and have my daughter learn to
live—on our own. I wish to heaven I were as low and
vile as you and that the dictates of conscience would
permit me to tell Father truthfully why I left my husband,
that you were sleeping with my husband for years. Your
artist. Your lover. My husband. I cannot, but I am writing
this to you so that you will not labor under the delusion
that you have bested or broken me. I cannot answer for
what you have done to my husband, but you have not
beaten me.

It will pain you to know that I did not leave my husband because I no longer loved him. Your having slept
with him did not change or alter my love for him one
whit. It will grieve you further to know that Anthony
and I always had a love like no other. I left him, quite
simply, because I could not look at him without seeing
your malignant hands all over him and I feared it might
be catching. I will go on loving him, but I will not go
on living with him and I certainly will not come back to
Belle Haven and live in any proximity to that very ma-
lignancy, however nicely you might clothe it in the veil
of respectability. Though I understand that your new
husband is a divorced man, and I wonder that Father
didn't cast you out for bringing scandal on the family as
he cast me out. But you always had a way with Father.
You convinced him to disinherit me and to forgive you.

So be it. You and Father, quite frankly, are two of a kind, lewd, bullying, and unscrupulous, and it will please me till my dying day that you may have got everything you wanted of life except for Anthony. You didn't get Anthony. He never loved you. He loved me and always will.

Julia Beale.

I watched it all go up in flame. All of it: my mother's pain and pride. My father's remorse. The fire devoured it all, just as desire had devoured them all. All except Charlotte. And she was probably being devoured by desire at this very minute, gasping about in the arms of that brute butler. I particularly pitied Favour at that moment—so easily cowed just because he had the body of a god and the mind of a child. This new butler had the body of a beast and the mind of a dog; he would not be so easily cowed, and if Charlotte thought so, it would be a grave and arrogant miscalculation. Of course Charlotte was arrogant and had reason to be: she'd cowed us all, the living and the dead, as well as the near dead if one were to include Bay's mother. Mrs. Margaret Hamilton never raised her voice and got everything she wanted—except for Bill Hamilton; she couldn't get Bill Hamilton back and she couldn't keep death from devouring her insides and Bay would not be free until death was done with her.

The love we made and gave and took in the boathouse that morning gave me some glimmer of hope for a future together, but I knew, as I stared at the curling, glowing embers, that I could not wait for Bay's mother to die. He was bound by filial obligation to stay until then and I was newly bound by filial obligation out of respect to my mother and father to leave at the earliest possible moment. Tomorrow. In light of what I now knew, I could not stay at Belle Haven any longer, even if I left without money or skills, without Bay Hamilton. I could no longer allow Charlotte Courtney the least say in the direction of my life. My pity for her evaporated when I reflected how she must have delighted in shaping my life with the likes of Merrywell College, where I learned nothing of any value except to make me an ornament, the dependent and inferior of the man she chose for my husband. Poor Ernest Emery. He was probably in debt to the top of his noble family tree and so in need of Charlotte's money that he didn't care that I came with it.

No, tomorrow I would take my leave of Belle Haven and find the highway. Past the highway, the future was a perfect terrifying blank. I would write to Bay Hamilton; such was the strength of our love, I was certain he would one day come to and for me, but for the present I was on my own. I pulled the shawl tight around me and closed my eyes and prayed, "Dear God—if you ever listen to Austin, who prays all the time, please hear me just this once. Give me the strength to leave this place. Wash me clean of Belle Haven." I fell asleep with the shawl about my shoulders, just as I sit now, seventy years later, the crone that lurks in every girl, the canker in every rose. I never thought I would live this long. I almost didn't.

16

I dressed warmly, in thick stockings, a dark wool skirt, a cotton blouse, a sweater, and a heavy coat. I carried a small suitcase packed with a few essentials and my sturdy walking shoes, so as not to arouse any of the troubled sleepers at Belle Haven. I closed the door to my room for the last time and tiptoed down the staircase. It was dark inside the house, though outside the first flecks of dawn peeled away from the night. In my handbag I carried fifteen dollars, fifty cents, every bit of my meager savings, but I intended to raid the petty cash drawer in the library, where I knew Charlotte kept considerable money. (In the second drawer on the left, the very drawer in fact where she'd told the county attorney she kept her gun.) I regretted the need to stoop to thievery, but didn't balk at it.

As I stood in the main hall with my hand on the library door, I glanced into the dining room and saw those fox's eyes peering at me, much as Charlotte might have peered at me had she known what I was about. In that eerie pale light trembling through the patio doors, the fox's stare unnerved me and I nearly forgot the money and bolted for the main door. The fox seemed to chortle nearly audibly at my presumption in thinking I could escape Belle Haven. I hated that fox's baleful gaze. I could not leave without, once and for all, meeting and destroying my enemy—at least the eyes of my enemy.

So I stole into the dining room, where I could hear the distant sounds of the stirring servants readying breakfast in the kitchen downstairs, and from the sideboard directly beneath the mural I opened a drawer and selected a massive bone-handled carving knife with a blade so sharp I winced. I gripped that knife and attacked the fox, dug out its gold glittering eyes, plucked out the eyes that had offended me, my mother and my father, Bay's mother and Bay's father, Favour and Austin and all the others. I slashed the fox's body and from the bleeding fox, without quite knowing what I was doing, I moved to the figures on horseback and ripped the knife through Charles Fairchild's broad breast and scratched the features from his face. So seductive was the destruction that I severed Charlotte's head from her body and her legs from her horse and stabbed the figures of Alicia and Francesca as well, hating them for their cupidity and stupidity and vanity; I sliced their jackets and horses and faces, I destroyed all the well-mounted denizens of Belle Haven, save for my mother. So unreasoning was the rage that this vandalism spawned in me and so gratifying was the satisfaction I took in it, I wished, I needed, I had to destroy Belle Haven as well. I reached high for the house at the top of the painting, but I could not pierce it with my knife. So I climbed on the top of the sideboard, stood up, and drove that knife into the heart of Belle Haven, stabbed and shredded Belle Haven so brutally I would not have been surprised to see blood spurt from the porticos, and it was there, as I was standing on the sideboard, knife poised in my hand, that Marian found me as she carried in a tray of polished silver and gleaming crystal;

though she could not scream, her mouth opened in a round, wordless shriek and the silver clattered to the parquet floor with a deafening crash.

Ethel came bounding up the stairs, her apron flying, with the young scullery maid right behind her. When they saw the shattered glass, the fallen silver, the slashed mural—and me, knife in hand, frozen in a tableau of guilt—Ethel and the scullery maid both screamed, though Ethel clapped her hand over her mouth and gave the maid a quick cuff and told her to shut up. She surveyed the scene quickly, noting my suitcase and shoes on the floor. "Running away, eh, miss?" She turned to the maid. "Get downstairs and pack up that ham and some fresh bread in a bag and be quick about it. Get!" She turned back to me. "I don't blame you, miss, not one bit. Belle Haven's no place for a young girl, especially not now, with that new butler. But you better get down and get out, miss. They might have heard the crash."

Marian helped me down from the sideboard and picked up my shoes and suitcase. Ethel's feet crunched over the broken glass and Marian led me around it and we were poised at the door that led downstairs to the kitchen when voices from the upstairs landing echoed down to us. Angry voices.

"Not that way, you fool. The other staircase. The servants' staircase," hissed Eugene desperately. "Do as I tell you."

"Tony Morona don't take no servants' staircase," came the gruff reply.

"Get back down with the rest of the servants. It's dawn, I tell you! Everyone will know."

A loud brutish laugh resounded and grew closer as Tony Morona sauntered down the length of the main staircase. "That's a good one. You think everyone don't know? Ha ha ha."

Ethel thrust me through the door and we clattered down the kitchen staircase. Overhead in the dining room we first heard Tony's heavy step and then his bellowing laughter, his coarse oaths as he stared at the mural.

"That'll do it," said Ethel, thrusting the bag of ham and bread into my arms. "They'll be down now for sure. Hurry, miss."

I hastily drew on my shoes and Marian darted to her room and came back with a wad of cash and stuffed it into my purse. "No, Marian, no. That's your savings. I can't. I won't."

Marian pushed the money back into the purse and snapped it shut, pointing at me, nodding fiercely.

"You take it, miss," said Ethel. "You pay Marian back sometime, but you'll need that money now. Make no mistake of it. Now, you'd best get." She pushed me towards the door and the chill of the dawn. "Don't go around front—go through the woods, around by the stables. The woods are thickest there and they won't see you and you can get to the highway. Good luck, miss."

I was perhaps half a mile from the house when I heard the dog yelping through the woods and I knew they'd unleashed Caesar on me. His barking and baying resounded through the trees. I ran on, making for the highway, but even at the highway, what was to prevent them from finding me? It would be deserted at dawn and I would be a conspicuous figure alone there on the road. The trees seemed to rattle with Caesar's anxious barking, more like twenty dogs than just one. I dropped the bag of food, hoping that would stall him, and I made through the underbrush and the thick woods, but the sounds of the dog and booted feet crashing through the woods pursued me, closer and closer, till I glanced at the dawn sky and realized—hoped, prayed, believed—that Bay might well be at the boathouse. Surely he would be there. He had to be there. We were lovers yesterday and today he would be back and save me.

I quickly took my bearings and altered my course north,

towards the lake. Panting, dripping with sweat, my face and arms scratched, I ran through the woods, dropping the suit-case and using both arms to clear the naked branches from my path. I fell time after time, but made my way towards the boathouse, running with Caesar still behind me. When finally I came to the edge of the lake I screamed Bay's name over and over again, stumbling towards the boathouse as my voice reverberated forlornly over the empty water. My very heart seemed to chant *Be There Be There* as I made my way around the lake towards the boathouse, which was as deserted as the water. Bay was not there, and I had no one to stand between me and certain capture. I threw my weight against the door and pressed against it sobbing, calling Bay's name as I heard Caesar and his companions drawing closer.

With one massive shove, the door gave way and I was hurled against the opposite wall. I lay there weeping while Caesar danced and barked around me and I stared into the boots of Eugene and Tony Morona.

Eugene patted Caesar and calmed him as his eyes adjusted to the half light and he stared into the open rafters where Bay and I had made our discoveries and our love. He ordered Anthony to get me off the floor. Anthony gripped my arm and pulled me to my feet and kept his iron fingers clenched around my flesh. Eugene (dressed only in his pants and braces and underwear) stood on the chair, just as Bay had, and hoisted himself through the opening into the rafters. I could hear him scuffling overhead.

"Let go of me, you ape." I tried to wrest my arm from Anthony's grasp, but he only held on tighter. I kicked him, and he said in a good-natured way that if I did that again he'd break my arm.

Twenty minutes later Eugene jumped back down from the rafters, dusting off his hands and brushing the dirt from his pants. A curious smile lit his bony face. "Charlotte's a crafty one, isn't she, Dabney? How did you find all this?"

"Go to hell and rot there," I replied. As if on cue, Anthony tightened his fingers round my arm.

Eugene came up to me and with a gesture of menacing tenderness, he brushed the hair back from my shoulders and wound his fingers through it. Then he yanked my head back with a jerk. His nose hairs quivered from his excitement. "Did you have a lovely time here, Dabney? A lovely summer? You and your doctor lover. He is your lover. You can tell me. I find it amusing, actually. I'm not surprised, of course. Plain women are often passionate. Perhaps more passionate than the great beauties."

"You're a snake, Eugene. You crawl on your belly."

He let go of my hair and grinned. "I could, Dabney. I could crawl on my belly up you." He ran his finger down my cheek and throat and rested it at the button of my blouse. "There's nothing to keep you from having more lovers, you know."

My knees went weak with terror and but for Anthony's grip I would have slid to the floor. I knew that in a minute I would be screaming, begging him to stop, not to touch me, not to hurt me.

"If you screamed no one would hear you, Dabney," he said, reading my thoughts.

"God would hear me," I said defiantly, knowing that God Himself could do nothing for me at this moment.

"No, Austin keeps God busy. There's just us three here and I want you to tell me about your doctor lover. Is he very clinical with you? His father was, you know—clinical, that is. Not at first. Charlotte has told me how at first he was hungry for her, at first he hungered for her body in ways she found quite novel. Is the son as hungry? Is the son as novel?" Eugene flicked open the first few buttons on my blouse and dipped his finger in and ran it round the tips of my breasts. I began to blubber and cry helplessly. Eugene undid another few buttons and my blouse gaped open. "I always thought Charlotte underestimated you, Dabney. It's good to hear you snivel and cry. Convinces me that you really are a woman. I wonder what it would take to convince Charlotte." He pulled the ribbons on my camisole and they knotted. Methodically he picked at the knot. "How amused do you think Charlotte will be to know you've found these nude paintings of her, executed by A.D.B. Your late, lamented father, if I'm not mistaken." The ribbons came loose and hung down, like long pink useless tongues.

He seemed to nod to Anthony, who abruptly tightened his grip on me; my back arched and I cried out again. Eugene smiled and his hairy fingers rested on my breasts and I heard Anthony grunt that he got a turn too, and then, though Anthony had hold of my body, at least I still had possession of my mind and I thank God that I remembered that Eugene Duckworth, scum that he was, had one tiny point of pride left and I cried out, "You must have come from a family of pigs to do this, you coward! All your ancestors were dogs! A race of dogs! The Duckworths must have crawled out of the swamp to have spawned a coward like—"

I got no further. Eugene slapped me full across the face and I thought I heard him mutter that I was not the one he was after, but I couldn't be sure because we left the boathouse then, Anthony following Eugene and dragging me, kicking, crying, screaming, fighting, back to Belle Haven.

Following Eugene we entered the house through the dining room and went thence into the library, where Charlotte stood in her mauve dressing gown beside the fire, her face alight with outrage, the very lace on her sleeves trembling.

Eugene closed the door firmly behind him and Anthony thrust me into the center of the room, where I tripped. I stayed on the floor, rubbing my aching arm. I quickly buttoned up my blouse and hugged my sweater and jacket tight across my chest.

"You may go now, Anthony," said Charlotte in a voice not quite her own.

"No," Eugene countermanded. "I think Anthony better stay."

"I don't want him here."

"We might need him."

"We'll call if we do."

"Anthony stays," said Eugene decisively.

Charlotte shrugged. Her dressing gown rustled as she took a seat and attempted to regain some of her old command. "Then let him be useful. Stoke up the fire, Anthony. It's cold in here."

Indeed it was. The cold and the rot of Belle Haven seemed to gather, and even the lively crackling of the now roaring fire could not banish it. I kept my eyes on the leaping flames while I heard Eugene telling her in his coolest, almost courtroom, tones that I was caught running away. I expected some sarcastic abuse from Charlotte, expected her to ask how I could have run away from lovely Belle Haven, just as she'd inquired of the county attorney when he asked why Favour would kill himself. But she was silent, her gaze shifting quickly between Eugene and me. The look in her eyes was not that of triumph and malice, like that of the fox in the dining room, but it was an animal look nonetheless: fear.

Eugene went on in cool, sardonic fashion, praising Caesar for his role in the chase, referring to me as a kind of quarry, finishing up with where he had found me. And moreover, what I had found there. "Some paintings of you, Charlotte. Quite nice paintings. Perhaps we should frame them and hang them in the dining room in place of the mural your niece has desecrated. Did you notice, Charlotte, that Dabney quite decapitated you?"

"Yes," said Charlotte tersely.

"I like the nudes better anyway. You were quite lovely in those days, Charlotte. It's a pity you're getting old and skinny."

"Stop it."

"Don't you think she's getting old and skinny, Anthony? Tell me who was the last woman you lay on whose hip bones pierced you?"

"Stop it, I told you."

"You're quite right, of course, my dear. Anthony's opinion of your body is hardly crucial to this discussion."

"Eugene, I want you to leave me alone with my niece. I shall deal with Dabney in my own way."

"A family matter, is that it, Charlotte?"

"Yes," she said crisply. "Exactly."

Eugene's bony face crinkled. "Am I not your family lawyer, Charlotte?" He sat down and carelessly tossed one knee over the other. "Do I not know everything there is to know about the Fairchilds? About you, Charlotte?"

"Don't flatter yourself, Eugene," she replied airily.

"Oh, I don't. I know why your father hired me. I know my place. I know it all the better now."

"Get out, Eugene, and take that ape with you."

Eugene lit up a cigarette with an exaggerated air of ease. Charlotte played nervously with the thick lace that fell from her elbows. I, having got my breath back and still clutching my heavy jacket across my chest, rose warily and moved towards the door. Eugene commanded me to sit.

"I'm not Caesar," I replied with more bravado than I felt. I had no wish to feel Anthony's paws on me again. "You can't—"

"Go sit in that chair and tell Charlotte what you found, Dabney. Tell her what you and your lover found. Oh, I forgot, Charlotte, did you know that your former husband's son has been honey-fucking your young niece, probably daily, am I right, Dabney? Hard to think of Dabney vamping the young doctor, isn't it, but she did. They're lovers. Doesn't that amuse you? I thought surely it would."

"Dabney could sleep with the dog. It's of no concern to me."

"Lie down with dogs, get up with fleas," I said to my own surprise, and in the corner Caesar snorted.

"I'm sure she found more than the paintings, didn't you, Dabney? Answer me, damn it!" Eugene commanded, though he never took his eyes off Charlotte.

"Yes."

"What else? Be specific," he said, as though I were a witness he was gently leading before a jury.

"Books."

"That's not all."

"That's all." I glanced over to Charlotte, who was staring straight ahead in a distracted manner totally foreign to her and for one moment I longed to go to her, to put my arms around her, to feel her old arrogance jolt through my body, to give strength as well as take it.

"Answer me, girl or you'll regret it. Anthony will make sure—"

"Letters."

"Ah. Letters." Smoke billowed out of his nose. "You have a great many dark, dirty little secrets, Charlotte, but I always knew there was something you wouldn't part with and—while I am no art critic, admittedly"—he looked at us as though he expected us to dispute this—"when I saw those paintings, I thought: that's it. Charlotte loved her sister's husband. You shock me, Charlotte."

"You hardly strike me as a moralist, Eugene."

"I don't give a damn for the morals of it. It's the principle. In principle, I would never have guessed you capable of love. You see, Dabney"—he turned to me, his cold eyes glittering—"Charlotte confuses love with all sorts of other things— sex, power, pain, gratification, money. Things like that. My great strength is that I am never confused. I have never been confused, Charlotte. Never."

Charlotte regarded Eugene as though seeing him for the first time, but she said nothing.

"Of course now I understand why you so hated your sister Julia. You had no respect for the other two—and of course they deserve none—but Julia, you loathed. You loathed Dabney, too, didn't you? For that very reason. You loved the painter Anthony Beale."

"I certainly hope you don't imagine that I'd ever have fallen in love with you, Eugene." She stood abruptly, swished over to the fire, held her hands there, warming them.

"I suspect there's more. You wouldn't have covered it up, so completely and for so long, if there wasn't more. What did the letters say, Dabney?"

"I'm not telling you anything, Eugene," I replied, taking my cue from Charlotte, but it was wrongly calculated, because Eugene merely nodded and Anthony was across the room. I was yanked from my chair and my arm bent behind me as it had been in the boathouse. I yelped with the pain.

Charlotte turned, covered her face with her hands, and stifled a moan.

"Ladies, you're—both of you—nothing but the barely legitimate spawn of a glue peddler. A carpetbagging panderer who had no right to any of this"—Eugene swept his hand around the library and flicked his butt into the fireplace. He advanced on me. "You will tell me what I want to know, Dabney, or I shall instruct Anthony to hurt you. He's very good. He's had lots of practice."

My arm jerked up again and Anthony's grip tightened against my ribs. I choked, sobbed, until I couldn't stand the pain and pressure any longer. "I know everything!" I cried. "I know about the abortion and Bay's father! I know what you did to my father, how you drove him to death and you drove Bay's father to death and you killed my mother and you've used me for revenge all these years! I know everything!" Anthony's grip on my ribs subsided. Slightly.

"How?" Eugene demanded.

"Letters."

"Where are they?"

"Burnt."

"You're lying."

"I burnt them!" I cried. "Let go of me!"

Charlotte lifted the lacy hem of her dressing gown and wiped her nose and eyes with it, and with that lowly gesture she seemed to recover herself. She leveled her gaze on Anthony as if she were aiming a rifle. "You will let go of my niece, Anthony. This instant."

Anthony chuckled and shook his head. His arm tightened round my ribs.

"He is a beast, Eugene. He's enjoying this."

"Aren't you, Charlotte?"

"I think the whole thing is revolting. If Dabney wants to run away, then let her. It's of no concern to me. Now let her go, Anthony." In her voice rattled an audible grain of fear. "Eugene, you will do as I tell you and tell him to let Dabney go."

"I've been doing what you tell me to for twenty years, Charlotte."

"He's hurting her."

"I noticed."

"What is it you want, Eugene?" she demanded.

"I want to watch you writhe, Charlotte. I want to see you blubber. I want to watch while that cool patrician demeanor of yours cracks and shatters into a million pieces, that demeanor that money bought you. Nothing else. You and your glue-peddling father, you ridiculous—" He went on and on, heaping abuse on the Fairchilds, using almost the same words he had used that day on the patio to me, only then he was cool and dispassionate and now the very catalogue of his ills and the Fairchild injustices drove him, as the past had driven him, long after lust and greed had failed. I feared for my life as I realized the depth—not of his depravity—I had guessed that—but of his hatred for us, for Charlotte in particular. He waxed on, wretchedly, vividly, and in the coarsest, most animal terms, describing how Charlotte must have felt when my father eloped with my mother, leaving her pregnant. "Now we'll hear it all from Dabney. Tell us, Dabney. Tell us all about Charlotte's abortion and her falling in love"—Eugene all but spat out the last word—"with some besotted paint pot of a second rate—"

There was a flash of mauve and for a moment I thought Anthony had hit me again, but it was Charlotte; she bolted, she flung herself on Anthony and me, pulled his hair, pummeled his face, shrieked, and told me to run, though pinned there beneath the two of them, I couldn't.

And then—I never quite knew how it happened—the library doors were flung open, and there stood Austin in his white pajamas, like an avenging angel, arms outthrust, his face popping red, his drunken voice rattling the very walls, "Thou whore! Thou shalt not injure one hair of her head! Destruction to the wicked! God's wrath shall not spare the wicked!" Austin hurled his huge gelatinous body into the fray with Charlotte and Anthony and me, and we thrashed on the floor; my lip cracked open and blood from Anthony's nose spewed over me. Austin kicked Charlotte, flung her off me, kicked her again, and she rolled against the marble fireplace. "Down with the whore and her whoremongering pimp!" I managed to pull myself out from underneath Anthony just before Austin grabbed hold of his head and smashed his face against the floor. Anthony bucked ferociously, knocked Austin off him, scrambled to his feet, and ran.

As I looked up, I saw to my horror that Charlotte's lacy sleeves had caught fire. She shrieked as the pale lace ignited the length of her arm and licked into her hair, and she ran, like a rocketing torch, screaming, at the same moment that

Austin, oblivious to her suffering, turned his wrath to Eugene, who stood seemingly frozen before us, a spectator until Austin grabbed a flaming stick that had tumbled from the fire. Clutching the scorched end of it in his unfeeling hand, he brandished the stick at Eugene, crying, "The fire! The corrupt shall be cast into the fire! Let the fire come down from heaven, let the wicked perish." He chased Eugene about the room, with Caesar snarling after them, and I seemed caught in a vortex of fire and shrieks, Austin and Charlotte, their fiery anguish and hatred torching the drapes, the overstuffed chairs and the books that lay everywhere around us, mounds of dry old paper that caught fire and billowed smoke and burst into angry, devouring flames.

I roused myself from the ground and caught at Charlotte as she tore past me. I dragged her to the ground and tried to pull the flaming dressing gown from her body, burning my hands and face and hair as she ran from me. I caught her charred outstretched hand and dragged her from the flaming library into the salon, where I rolled her, screaming and reeking of burned flesh, into the Persian carpet, but smoke choked us as Austin, still waving his flaming brand, pursued Eugene into the salon. It was then I realized that Austin was actually deliberately torching the drapes and paintings, so everything would burn. I pulled and tugged at the heavy carpet, struggled till I'd moved it to the window, where I smashed the glass with my feet and pulled the rug and Charlotte through the broken glass after me, rolled her into the cold November morning, into the dank, dying grass, until we came to rest at the foot of one of the massive ginkgo trees, with their soft, flesh-colored berries stinking everywhere around us on the ground.

Smoke poured from the windows of Belle Haven and I looked up to see Austin, torch in hand, framed in the flaming draperies of one of the upper windows. He stood with his arms upraised to heaven and cried out to God to witness the destruction of Belle Haven and then he turned and walked back into the very hell he'd wrought.

I could not watch Belle Haven burn, but as I heard the upper stories crash and give way, I knew we would not be safe by the ginkgo tree when the house collapsed. So I held Charlotte wrapped in the carpet in my arms, talking to her, getting no reply, promising I'd save her as, half running, half tumbling, I fell down the broad, coarse lawn, pulling the carpet, rolling it, carrying, dragging it the last few steps till at last I—we— fell into the ravine that fronted the highway, and into the muddy creek that lay like a shallow seam at its bottom. I knelt there in the cold water and gently peeled the rug back from my aunt's body. The stench of burned flesh and hair rose like a plume. Her skin was everywhere charred and blackened, but her eyes were alive: the fox's eyes of the mural—meeting death with unstilled arrogance. I wept as I dipped my hand into the water and dribbled some over her lips. She pressed her tongue against her teeth. "You're so like your father," she whispered.

"Hush, please, Charlotte," I begged her. "Save your strength, Charlotte."

Gentle derision lit her eyes momentarily. "Both fools," she mumbled, "brave, beautiful fools."

Part III

17

I waited to be interviewed in Miss Baum's office. I sat in one of the diminutive wooden chairs facing her desk; the chair was clearly molded for a child's body and I felt small and quite helpless. A miscreant student called into the principal's office at Flintridge School would have scant chance here. Behind the desk hung an aged, outdated map of the United States, flanked on either side by pictures of Robert E. Lee and Jefferson Davis. Rows of black Bibles lined the bookshelves, along with thick texts on history and religion. The windows were curtainless and gave a Spartan view of the walls of Flintridge, a few old trees, the meager grounds all blanketed with snow. So bleak was the outlook that January's very fingers crept into the room, despite the glowing small stove in the corner.

I rose when Miss Baum entered. She was a middle-aged woman, clearly of severe habits and set ideas, wearing a shapeless black dress of cheap material. Little pins stuck out from the bun at the top of her head, reminding me oddly of the Statue of Liberty. Miss Baum, however, was no apostle of freedom. Quite the contrary.

"Take a seat, Miss Beale. Normally we would not have an

opening in midyear, but one of our teachers left unexpectedly to get married. At least"—Miss Baum's mouth twitched—"I hope that's what she intends to do."

I nodded, but said nothing.

She surveyed me critically. "I must be frank, Miss Beale. I disapprove of bobbed hair. Disapprove of it entirely."

"It wasn't my choice. I was in an accident, a fire, and it was singed. It will grow back."

"Yes. I must say, you don't have the look of robust health. Your hands—"

I wound my scarred hands in my lap. "I'm quite healthy now. That was months ago."

"I don't know, Miss Beale. The task of teaching responsibly is enough to tax the sturdiest constitution. I do not wish to have to interview someone else in a month's time because you have collapsed on me."

"I welcome the prospect of hard work. It will make me stronger, not weaker. I will not collapse."

Miss Baum toyed with a pencil with a saber-sharp point. "I am impressed with your credentials, Miss Beale." She followed down the list of educational institutions I'd attended, checking each one with her pencil. "Most of our teachers come from considerably less illustrious backgrounds, downstate normal schools; some have no advanced education at all. You, on the other hand, have been to Miss Blackwell's Academy, Miss Hunter's School for Girls, the Portland School, even, I see here, Merrywell College. I am a Merrywell alumna, Class of Ninety-five. I was a charity student there. Were you a charity student, Miss Beale?"

"No."

"I thought not. Why do you wish to teach at Flintridge, Miss Beale?"

"I need the job. I am penniless." I replied.

"I see." She snapped her mouth shut like a frog with a

choice fly and studied my list again. "You did not graduate
from Merrywell?"

"No."

"May I ask why?"

"A family tragedy intervened."

"Your father lost his money, something like that?"

"Something like that."

"I see," she said snapping her mouth shut again. "At Flintridge we strive for literacy. Literacy. Cleanliness. Promptness,
obedience, and rectitude, Miss Beale, rectitude in all things.
We endeavor to fit our students to take up useful occupations
in the world, to go forth as Christian examples, missionaries,
teachers, or wives; whatever their path in life, they must fulfill
their Christian obligations. As I recall, these were not the
sort of attributes stressed at Merrywell College."

"No, but Merrywell was very fond of rectitude, Miss Baum,
you must remember that, very fond indeed."

"Very well, Miss Beale, you may begin your duties tomorrow. You will be in charge of the fourth-year students.
The undermatron will show you to your room." She rang a
little bell and the undermatron, a wizened, rumpled little
gnome of a woman, appeared. "We take our breakfast
promptly at seven," Miss Baum announced. "Prayers are at
seven-thirty, school begins at eight-thirty. Dinner is served
at noon and classes resume at twelve-thirty. At four o'clock
we have a daily convocation for prayers and punishments, if
there are any to be meted out. Then we encourage our students to do a bit of walking or reading or whatever most suits
them. Within reason, of course. Supper is at six, followed by
evening prayers. Lights out for the students at eight, at nine
for the faculty. Is all that clear?"

"Yes, Miss Baum."

"Welcome to Flintridge, Miss Beale."

Welcome to Flintridge, indeed. Christ Himself would not

have lingered at Flintridge. The rooms were drafty and cold, the beds hard, the blankets thin, the grounds were cheerless, the chapel was spare, the meals unappetizing; the staff was pious and restrained in all things, and the students were crass, churlish, and understandably unwilling to learn. But I did welcome Flintridge—the long hours, the hard work, even the grim regime all helped to banish Belle Haven from my waking hours. The nights, however, gave me no peace or freedom. I lay awake on my narrow cot, watching the cold moonlight stalk the bare, small room and reliving the burning of Belle Haven.

Charlotte had died there in my arms, though I did not know it. Indeed, I did not even know how long, for how many hours, I sat in that muddy creek holding her, sobbing, railing. I may even have lost consciousness altogether, for my only clear recollection was the eventual cry of dogs and light: lanterns coming downhill like giant, impossible fireflies in the early dusk. And voices. Men's voices. The sound of boots and men trying to pry the carpet from my arms, blankets thrown over me, and then Bay's voice breaking through all the rest. At Bay's voice, I let go of the carpet that held Charlotte's body. I let go of everything.

I awoke in a Lynchburg hospital (Oakstone has no hospital) and I stayed there for a week, till Dr. Pruitt and his wife came to take me to their home. For all their priggishness, the Pruitts were very good to me. The doctor tended to my burns as though I were his own daughter and they told me I could stay with them as long as I liked.

We did not, however, go directly to their home, as it was the afternoon of the funeral for Charlotte and Austin, and over the Pruitts' objections I insisted on going. Actually there wasn't enough of Austin to bury, so they gathered up some ashes from Belle Haven in an urn and buried it symbolically with Charlotte—in her coffin, ironically. Austin would at last share a bed with her, the last bed of all.

Alicia told me they would put both names on the headstone when the time came. Both she and Francesca were there, having hastened to Virginia when the dreadful news caught up with them in New York. When they saw me—Dr. Pruitt pushing me in my wheelchair, great mittens of bandages around my hands and arms, my face scarred (and indeed, I would have been more badly burned save for my heavy coat and sweater), my hair cut in an impromptu bob and still singed and grizzled—they both burst into tears.

"Oh, Dabney!" cried Francesca. "Charlotte would have understood that you were too ill to come to her funeral."

The hell she would, I thought. But I went to the funeral not for Charlotte, not even for Austin, whom I was very fond of, but because there were two pairs of eyes I wanted to meet: Bay Hamilton's and Eugene Duckworth's.

Eugene had escaped. Everyone escaped, save for Charlotte and Austin. Anthony bolted and was not seen or heard from again. The servants eventually all found employment in other great houses in the vicinity. (Marian, in fact, was absorbed into the Emery household, no doubt because, being mute, she came more cheaply than the others.) And no doubt too, the former servants percolated their tales of life at Belle Haven through the basement corridors of their new homes, nasty subterranean little secrets that seldom surfaced upstairs in the well-lit salons or manicured gardens.

The funeral was attended by the cream of local society, as well as by the merely curious, those same sorts who crowded round Belle Haven when Favour died. Eugene stood alone and aloof, dressed in cindery black, his hair (like mine) singed and grizzled. He wore no bandages, carried no visible scars. I never knew how he escaped Austin's wrath or the flaming torch with which Austin had pursued him through the house. Eugene looked somber, if not quite grieving. Alicia and Francesca stood nearby him, weeping loudly, their puffy faces blanketed in cosmetics and grief. They wore stylishly cut mourning clothes and wept on the shoulder of any male who proffered a hand in sympathy.

So, as Dr. Pruitt wheeled me through the crowd, I saw everyone (including that insufferable bean-brained Marjorie Vail) but Bay Hamilton. I blamed Bay. For everything. *If he had been there, that fateful morning at the boathouse, if he had been waiting for me as he should have been, would have been if he'd truly loved me, none of this . . .* The pain of these reflections hurt far worse than anything bandaged on my body. Dr. Pruitt halted at the graveside and the minister was about to begin his farewells to Charlotte and Austin when a small boy raced up to me and asked if I was Miss Dabney. "A man give me a whole quarter if I was to deliver this to you, miss." And he thrust in my lap a single red rose. So completely bandaged were my hands I could not even lift it. Dr. Pruitt inquired after the man, but the boy did not know his name. I did, but I did not know what the rose stood for. Was it an excuse? A plea for forgiveness? Or simple admission that Bay Hamilton was human, had acted at the behest of his loins, made love to a girl who had flung herself at him, even though he had never really loved her. Who could blame him? Would Marjorie Vail blame him, I wondered, as I glanced beyond the grave that would hold Charlotte and Austin. "Oh," I said aloud, "of course." The stone next to Charlotte's grave said *William Bayard Hamilton.* Where else would they have buried the Doctor? He had chosen Belle Haven in life and he would lie there with the Fairchilds in death. But his son would not be at this funeral, this public occasion, complete with gawkers and the old resurrected scandals.

"Darling Dabney." Francesca came up to me afterwards and knelt at the foot of the wheelchair and took my bandaged hands in hers. "You tried so hard to save her. They found you with her in your arms, darling Dabney," she said and wept.

Alicia joined her and put her hands on my shoulders. "Of course Charlotte was the closest thing to a mother you've had all these years."

Milling mourners joined them, encircling my wheelchair. One would have thought me the corpse for all the attention I attracted. They all commented on my futile heroic attempts to save my aunt and on my wounds, received in such a noble cause. Of course the bruises on my face had nothing to do with pulling Charlotte from the fire; they were the gift of Anthony, but no one mentioned Anthony—he might as well never have lived, so completely was he eradicated from tales of the Belle Haven fire.

I watched Eugene at the edge of the crowd, hat in hand, the chill November wind ruffling his coat, the tombstones around him like a troupe of admiring dwarfs. People offered him condolences too and reassured him of his good fortune in having survived the catastrophe.

Yes, I overheard him saying, faulty wiring somewhere . . . the electrical circuits were added after the house was built and they were never quite right . . . yes, Austin was too drunk to be roused, and yes (he said with a sigh), Charlotte would have preferred death to disfigurement.

And then as the crowd thinned and the mourners returned to their own lives, Eugene approached me. He nodded to Dr. Pruitt and asked after my health and Pruitt gave a hearty imitation of a laugh. "Oh, she's young, Mr. Duckworth, she's in splendid health and it's just a matter of time before she recovers."

"She's a brave little girl, Dr. Pruitt, a plucky little heroine, isn't she? She'll soon get on with things, bury the past and get on with our lives, eh, Dabney?"

"You have the soul of a toad," I replied unequivocally and to the almost mortal shock of the Pruitts, "and you are a coward and all your ancestors *were* dogs and I wish to heaven you'd burnt to death instead of Austin and Charlotte."

He turned and walked away and I never saw Eugene Duckworth again.

I was informed of the reading of the will, but I declined to attend. Besides, I knew the outcome. Alicia and Francesca went to his office that day and afterwards they rushed to the Pruitts' house. They burst into the parlor, full of indignation and surprise. "I don't believe it. I simply can't. Dabney dear, this will come as an awful shock," Alicia consoled me, "but you must try to be brave."

"She left everything to Eugene, didn't she?"

"Why! How did you know?"

"I guessed."

"I can't believe it. How could she have been so cruel? If only she could have known how you would struggle to save her life!"

Mrs. Pruitt brought us a tray of tea and beaten biscuits with thin-sliced ham. Francesca and Alicia waited for her to leave the room before discussing the awful family business at hand.

"I think you should contest it," Alicia continued. "There's not a judge in this county who wouldn't grant you something of the estate, not after what you've done."

"I don't want anything from it or from her."

"Well, dear, you say that now, but don't be too hasty."

"Why would Charlotte have left everything to Eugene?" Francesca helped herself to two lumps of sugar.

"Well, my dears—entre nous—I wonder if she did. That Eugene is a slippery creature, I've always thought so, and he was her lawyer and he might well have—I mean, let us be frank, he signed her name to documents all the time. I think that will is a fake."

"Oh no, Alicia. He wouldn't have done that. Eugene was in love with Charlotte. He'd never stoop to that." Francesca cooled her tea with a silver spoon.

"He might. He might very well and you know it."

"Even so, Charlotte was no fool. Charlotte knew everything about her own business—and our business as well. She never left decisions up to others, not even to Eugene, and if she left her entire estate to Eugene, well, we'll just have to trust her judgment, much as we might decry it. I think she gave it to him for twenty years of loving, loyal servitude."

"Then you are a fool, Francesca," Alicia retorted. "Well, at least we don't have to come back to Belle Haven and see Eugene Duckworth living there. That's one mercy. I don't think I could bear it."

"Papa would reel in his grave," Francesca concurred. "Eugene's selling Belle Haven, Dabney, did you know? Not the house of course, that's gone, but all the property. Our precious childhood home—sold." Francesca put her cup down to dab at her eyes. "He's already got a buyer."

"Already?" I asked, surprised at his alacrity. "Who?"

"A girls' school. Some wealthy New Yorkers have bought it and they're going to turn it into a college for girls and Eugene has agreed, but he's stipulated that they must name it Belle Haven College. Now, that has a nice ring, don't you think?"

"Won't Merrywell be furious!"

Alicia and Francesca giggled like girls. I listened to them weakly, their voices losing fiber and cadence. A school for girls, indeed. I wondered then and wondered still as I lay on my cot at Flintridge what troubled ghosts might haunt the dreams of the young ladies of Belle Haven College.

The girls at Flintridge suffered no such ghosts. They wrestled with no angels or devils. They fought off only chilblain and indigestion and insufferable crushing religion, much worse than anything Austin could have dreamed of—it lacked the drama and pathos of Austin's religion, and certainly the Song of Solomon had no place in Flintridge's version of the

Bible. We knelt on cold floors and thanked God for our many blessings and asked of Him only that we might be forged into His humble servants.

I taught reading, writing, sums, geography, history, deportment, and government to girls about the age of ten, some the daughters of clerical households, but most sent to Flintridge by well-meaning lower-class mamas who mistakenly perceived in Flintridge an opportunity for their daughters to rise in the world. The students were often and easily cowed—and those who were not vanished from Flintridge as soon as their incorrigible propensities made themselves known. So, as the months passed, every interesting child was whittled from my class and I was left with the sullen, the mentally destitute, and the snide.

My days were dreary and ill paid, but I always sent a portion of my salary to Marian to make up for her savings, which had been burned in the fire. I cannot say that I enjoyed the work or that it sufficed to still the pictures that would form unwillingly, persistently, relentlessly at the edge of my mind: the fire, the funeral, Favour, Charlotte dead in my arms, Bay alive in my arms the day before. I often unwillingly reconstructed that November dawn in every detail, winding my way through a boxwood maze of dreadful memory back to the boathouse, to Bay and our day of lovemaking. I knew I had to will myself to forget and I truly tried, but still I savored that memory, preserved in its perfect amber dawn. At least, I often thought, as I surveyed Miss Baum and the other gray teachers at our grim table, set with gray plates and grim food, at least I had a moment of passion to my credit. At least I am not like them.

Within a week of the funeral, Francesca and Alicia had left—Francesca to struggle with the British divorce laws and Alicia to a friend's yacht in the Aegean. I stayed at the Pruitts', gathering strength, hobbling out of the wheelchair, performing little household tasks for the Pruitts. By the hour I held up the yarn in my bandaged hands while Mrs. Pruitt wound up balls for her knitting. She chattered amiably, never requiring response from me. She seemed only to dread silence or the mention of Belle Haven.

"Look at that, Dabney," she said as she walked to the parlor window one morning. "The first snow." She pulled the curtain aside and surveyed her front garden proudly. "It can get tiresome about February, but the first snow puts such a lovely mantle on things, don't you think? A gentle quilt over suffering. I always warn the Doctor, wear your woollies now, Edgar, that's what I say, every year. Wear your woollies or you'll be making house calls on yourself, Edgar. But does he listen? No, that man works his fingers to the bone, he does, he . . ."

And on and on. I held the wool and peered out the window to the sycamore and the picket fence and the shriveled bushes all draped in gleaming white. Snowflakes clung to the window momentarily before sliding down like the tears of children. Beyond the window and the yard, as the snow fell I could see a dark figure emerging. A man's figure. I recognized his body before I ever saw his face. Oddly enough I felt no leap of the heart, no quickening of the senses. Only a mild curiosity, and a pervasive sadness.

". . . Oh, there's the door. Who would be out in weather like this? They'll freeze at the door before Annie gets there. She's getting old, you know, and she isn't as quick on her feet. Well, I guess none of us are, but well, excuse me, dear." Mrs. Pruitt bustled into the hall, calling out to Annie that she would get the door.

Bay Hamilton brought with him into that parlor a breath of snow, cold, and freshness, his skin enlivened by pulsating blood, human warmth, his eyes darkened with longing and chagrin. I rose unsteadily to my feet.

"Why Dabney, dear," Mrs. Pruitt said, "it's Dr. Hamilton. Just come to see how you're doing, I'll warrant. You're our

illustrious patient, that's what we call you, Dabney, the heroine of Belle Haven. And Doctor, a braver little girl you've
never seen. You see, Dabney, your fame has spread."

"Hello, Bay."

"Hello, Dabney."

Our first names must have momentarily struck Mrs. Pruitt
as odd. People might have been baptized with Miss, Mr., and
Mrs. for all she knew, but then a shadow crossed her face
and she must have remembered the Belle Haven ball and my
having slapped Dr. Hamilton in full view of the hundreds of
guests. "Oh dear," she fluttered. "Well, really, Dr. Hamilton,
Dr. Pruitt isn't in just now, but if you care to wait in his
office, I'm sure—"

"I've come to see Dabney, Mrs. Pruitt."

"It's quite all right, Mrs. Pruitt. Really. Could we have a
bit of privacy?"

"Privacy? The two of you alone together? Well"—she
frowned—"I guess it's all right. He is a doctor. Shall I bring
some tea?"

"No thank you."

She made a great fuss of picking up her knitting and left.

"How are you feeling, Dabney?"

"As well as can be expected."

He approached me tentatively and took my hands. "Do
you think Dr. Pruitt would mind if I took off the bandages
and checked your hands?" He unwound the bandages and
surveyed the hands wordlessly, then tied them back up.
"They're healing nicely. You might not even have scars. Not
bad ones, anyway."

"I'll have scars," I said.

We both sat down and stared at each other across the abyss
of the catastrophe.

"You know why I didn't come to the funeral," he said at
last.

I want to know why you didn't come to the boathouse. "I saw your father's headstone." That was all I said.

"I heard the news." Bay looked at me expectantly and so I obliged him and asked what news. "Everyone in this county knows that Charlotte Courtney did not leave you a cent."

"Her last revenge on my father, I guess."

"Only if it's true, Dabney. Lots of people think that Duckworth doctored the will to suit himself, so everything was left to him, and if you wanted, you could very easily contest—"

"I don't care who gets it. I don't care about Eugene and I don't care about the property or the money or anything. I feel only pity for Charlotte and that's all I feel. I'm sick unto death of the word *if*."

"If what?"

I met his gaze with a kind of uncaring candor. I had so often been over the events of that day, waking, sleeping, thinking, dreaming, that in some ways his reply scarcely mattered anymore. Nothing much mattered anymore. I said, "If you had been at the boathouse that morning. Everything would have been different. I tried to run away and they used the dog on me and I ran to the boathouse because I was sure you would be there at dawn and you would—"

"God help me, Dabney! I would have been! I was up all night in the country with a very difficult birth. I couldn't leave that woman at dawn."

"But you could leave me to the likes of Eugene!"

His face suddenly darkened. "I'll kill him if he hurt you, Dabney."

"Oh, Bay. Everybody's hurt me. I hurt all over. I'll hurt forever."

Bay bolted to my side, knelt, and wrapped his arms around me. "I would have been there, darling, oh Dabney, my love, nothing could have kept me away, but my patient—"

"I don't give a damn for your patient! And I don't believe you." I began to cry. "All you wanted was the stuff from Belle Haven and you never did want me or love me. I just flung myself at you like a fool and so, why shouldn't you—"

"No. No, Dabney. I left as soon as I could, as soon as I knew the mother and child would both live, and I drove straight into Oakstone and even from Oakstone I could see the smoke from Belle Haven, but by the time I got there the whole house was ablaze and all that the volunteer firemen could do was try to contain it so the woods didn't go up too. The servants had escaped and I ran around asking everyone about you, but no one had seen you. Finally I found Eugene with Dr. Pruitt and Eugene told me you were still in the house." Bay held me even tighter. "Oh Dabney, I was crazy with grief and fear and I begged the sheriff and some of the men to help me look for you anyway, hoping, praying—there was a dozen of us looking. One man sighted you and we heard the dogs—don't you remember, Dabney? I was the one who lifted you out of the water, out of the creek? Don't you remember?"

"No. Yes. I guess I knew you were there. I don't know anything for sure."

We sat, our heads together, arms around each other, and though we could hear Mrs. Pruitt's occasional anxious tread outside the door neither of us moved. Bay stroked my short hair, and I stayed close to his collar and the familiar smell of his skin. Finally I released myself from his embrace, rose, and unsteadily made my way to one of the wing chairs.

Bay sat silently, shifting his gaze from my eyes to his own hands. "The boathouse survived, you know. The whole house perished, but the fire never got as far as the boathouse. I took that as a sort of omen. A good omen."

"It doesn't matter. Everything burnt. Everything. Something of me died in that fire."

"Do you love me? That's the only question worth asking. Do you love me, Dabney?"

"I'm all burnt up inside. You can see it on the outside, but it's on the inside, too. It's worse inside."

"None of that matters."

"It does to me."

"The scars—none of it matters to me—I love you, Dabney. I will always love you."

"I'm going away, Bay. As soon as I can."

"How can you think of leaving me? We've only just found each other and now—"

"What would you have me do? Live here with the Pruitts and wait for your mother to die? Ghoulish. No, I'm going away altogether. I'll put as many miles as I can between me and Belle Haven, between me and that fire, between me and the past."

"And knowing I love you more than heaven and earth, that doesn't make any difference to you?" he demanded.

I rested my eyes on his beautiful face. "It doesn't change anything."

"Dabney, listen to me, don't do this, I beg of you, Dabney—the burning of Belle Haven freed us to love each other, freed us from Charlotte and the past—"

"Did it? What would your mother think if you were to marry a girl from Belle Haven? Would that ease her dying days?" The look on his face was reply enough. I asked if he had shown her his father's suicide note.

"No. I burnt them both myself, but I told her they must have perished in the fire."

"The destruction of Belle Haven must have given her enormous pleasure."

"She's too sick to take pleasure in anything. She isn't as vindictive as you think."

"No, I'm sure she's not. I know exactly how she feels. I'm

young, but I feel old, like all emotion is in the past." I was suddenly bone-weary, sick of it all. End this, I told myself. "Belle Haven's burning covered our love in cinder and ash. I taste it. Everytime I say your name, I taste it." I did not add that I went on saying his name in spite of the taste. I stood up and started for the door, but Bay caught me in his arms and I could tell from his voice and his eyes that he wanted to shake and throttle me, hold me tight up against him and only his concern for my fragile health prevented him from doing just that.

"My darling Dabney, don't do this. No one will ever love you like I do. I love you and I can't live without you."

"I know that. No one will ever love you like I—did, when I could love, when I could feel"—I squirmed out of his embrace—"anything at all."

"Didn't that morning in the boathouse mean anything to you?" he said fiercely. "Didn't the whole summer mean anything to you?"

I said very clearly and truthfully, "You made me as happy as I have ever been, Bay. As happy as I will ever be."

"And you can still tell me you don't love me anymore!"

I held out my white-swathed arms and hands. "Please, if you love me, just let me go. Don't make me talk anymore. I can't talk anymore."

I left him there in the Pruitts' parlor and went slowly upstairs to the little room they'd given me. I stood at the window and through the curtains of lace and snow, I watched his dark figure retreat till he was utterly enveloped in the snow and had vanished from my view.

18

Spring came to Flintridge unwillingly. In contrast to the gracious seasonal progress at Belle Haven, at Flintridge scrawny blossoms appeared on the trees, the tight-fisted buds opened with only a modicum of drama, and the winter skulked from our premises only when chased. As the second term drew to a close, talk at the teachers' table centered mainly on summer plans. Most of the teachers were returning to one home or another, and as they talked I pictured their picketed homes with dreary fathers intoning dreary prayers over dreary meals, and dreary mothers cleaning out grease cans and plucking eggs from the feathered underbellies of chickens.

"Where will you go, Miss Beale?" a Miss Scranton inquired of me one evening.

I picked at my cold bread and hash and regarded the half-dozen gray faces around me. "I have an aunt yachting in the Aegean," I said. "I may join her."

They laughed and glanced furtively at Miss Baum, who did not encourage frivolity of any sort.

The next day I went to Miss Baum's office and inquired if I might stay at Flintridge through the summer. "I have no place to go and no money anyway," I said. "I could perhaps be of service here."

"No aunt in the Aegean, Miss Beale?" she asked with as much sarcasm as someone like Miss Baum could muster. I was silent. "Only the undermatron and I stay the summer at Flintridge. We keep to no schedule. You'd have to get your own meals in the kitchen and take them alone. It will not be a pleasant place for a young woman. In the summer," she added, as if she knew I was thinking it was not a pleasant place for a young woman in any event. "But yes, if you wish to stay and be useful, you may. I could probably pay you quarter salary. No more."

"That will be fine."

"You've done quite well here, Miss Beale. Better than I expected."

"Thank you, Miss Baum."

No lake, no boats; indeed, no lover that summer, but I was my own mistress and my time was not spoken for. In a trunk I found some workingman's pants and a pair of heavy boots and I lived in them. I planted a small garden—tomatoes, squash, peas, beans—and took pride in its progress. I whitewashed the classrooms, and in the summer's golden afternoon light they glowed unexpectedly. I sanded and varnished all the desks, amused and touched occasionally by the childish messages secretly carved on them. (I was in fact rather heartened by the number of such messages, because anyone caught defiling school property was summarily dismissed.) I found some plaster and old brick and repaired the crumbling wall around the school's chicken yard. At night I read books from our meager collection and eventually reorganized and properly catalogued the library. Occasionally I went into Flintridge village, where I found a barber who was willing to trim my hair back into a comfortable bob. I had scant contact with Miss Baum, and when she saw my freshly cut hair, she let it pass without comment.

One day in August as I was redigging the water trenches around my tomatoes, I saw her approach. She complimented me on the garden, and since our exchanges were so few and perfunctory I expected her to walk on, but she stayed to discuss the garden and then, in the flat, white heat of noon, she offered, "You'll ruin your complexion out here in midday, Miss Beale."

"My complexion is already ruined."

"I can see that." She stared pointedly at the scars that trailed up my wrists and arms in long jagged patches. "I didn't realize your arms were scarred as well as your hands. I'm passing no judgments," she added quickly.

"Just inquiring?"

"Not out of malice, Miss Beale. Don't mistake my interest for that. Your hair's lightened considerably since you've been working outside and the color in your face has improved, though in general I think a milk complexion is best, don't you?"

"Only on cows."

"Speaking of cows, Miss Beale, I stumbled across a bit of news that might interest you. I went to Richmond last week."

"Did you? I hadn't noticed."

"I told you it would be lonely here in the summer."

"I'm not complaining, Miss Baum."

"I went to Richmond and I happened to see an old college friend from my Merrywell days—not a friend, really; charity students did not have friends, but a lady I knew there told me the most extraordinary story. She said a girl had actually been expelled last year for bringing a cow into the library and pushing it up to the second floor. Did that happen while you were there?"

"I don't think so. I would have remembered."

"You left before that—your father lost his money or something?"

"Something."

"And the fire—" she nodded towards my arms—"when did the fire occur? Before or after you left Merrywell?"

"After."

"Indeed? Have you heard, Miss Beale—they're starting a new women's college upstate, Belle Haven College. Have you thought of applying there for work? It might be more your style. I would certainly give you first-rate references."

"Thank you, Miss Baum, but I'm quite happy where I am."

"They're building the school over the ruins of an estate that burned last winter—a terrible fire that killed two people and injured one other."

"I'm happy where I am," I repeated.

"That's good to know, Miss Beale." And with that she strode into the building, a peculiar and disconcerting smile on her thin lips.

When the new term began I returned to my serviceable, long-sleeved dresses and my classroom. The autumn's melancholia attacked me with particular ferocity as I watched my garden die and the world sizzle up in flame and glory. I thought of the previous autumn and all the autumns to come and knew that all flame and glory were past for me, and whatever guilty pleasure I had taken from my love affair with Bay receded; I regarded my fellow teachers with less arrogance, more compassion—no doubt each of them had a buried love somewhere. How else could they have endured life at Flintridge if they hadn't something to look back on? They certainly had little to look forward to.

The chill of November again beset us and the whitewashed walls that had glowed in the summer sun seemed now only to reflect the arctic cold. I took to wearing fingerless mittens, partly for the cold and partly because they disguised my hands, which often elicited garish stares from the students. I was at the blackboard one morning, my very breath frosting before me as I parsed sentences for the benefit of my class, when Miss Baum entered. Her presence was enough to stiffen every backbone in the room. I could feel the students' collective rigor before I so much as saw Miss Baum.

"I'll take over here, Miss Beale. You're wanted in my office."

"Wanted?"

"Yes, Miss Beale. Now, make haste. God smiles on alacrity in all things. Isn't that right, children?"

"Yes, Miss Baum," they answered in dreary unison.

So I made haste, down the damp chill hall to Miss Baum's office, less curious than frightened by her intrusion into my classroom. (Miss Baum entered the classroom only in the event of death or dementia—both of which had been known to occur at Flintridge.)

I opened the door and was greeted by a gust of warm air from the stove, and standing before Miss Baum's desk I beheld Dr. Bayard Hamilton. "What are you doing here?" I asked as I closed the door quickly and leaned against it. "Do you want to get me sacked?"

"I told her I was an old family friend."

"And what did she say?"

"She said I wasn't that old."

He looked older. The gray that had salted his hair last year had crept into his beard. But then, I thought, I look older too no doubt—what with my chalky mittens, my dusty black skirt, chapped lips, and bobbed hair. "Why did you come? How did you find me?"

"I've brought you a letter and some news." He handed me a crumpled stained envelope with my name written carelessly across it. I opened it, and in the same hurried, barely literate hand I read:

Dear Miss Dabney—
It was me told Dr. Hamilton where you are. Don't be mad at him for coming and don't be mad at me for telling.
I never thank you for sending money. It wasn't yore

fault my money burnt up at Belle Haven. It would have burnt up even if I hadn't give it to you. But I took yore money because I am getting on and I been happy at the Emerys, but I don't have no wish to die in there service.

I went to Dr. H when I got a big lump on my hand. A sist he calls it. The Emerys wanted me to go to Pruitt, but after what he done to Mr. Austin time and time again, I wouldn't take nothing from him and besides I wanted to see Dr. H because, you'll forgive me Miss, but I knew you was seeing him that last summer at Belle Haven and that fall when poor James died by his own hand. You don't work at Belle Haven thirty years and not know what goes on.

Dr. H is a good man, Miss, a fine man and you couldn't do no better. You deserve your happiness, Miss. Your mother deserved hers and didn't get it, poor angel, but don't let that stop you. Don't you let nothing stop you miss. You take your happiness and don't let pride or Charlotte Courtney or nothing stop you. Your mother kept her pride and it cost her her life and you know it did. Aint no body to care what you take to the grave— pride or sin or goodness, it all comes to the same dust. You just think of Charlotte Courtney. All them people weeping and moaning over her when you and I know she had a soul as dark as boot blacking.

Maybe it's only the old folks think of these things, Miss. The grave's a long way off for you. You got a lot of years and I want you to be happy. If I didn't think Dr. H could give you happiness, I'd never told him where you are.

I never wrote anything this long in all my life.

God bless you, Miss Dabney.

Marian.

I tucked the letter in my pocket without comment. "And the news?" I said crisply.

"Eugene Duckworth is dead. He committed suicide."

I sank to one of the diminutive chairs and covered my face with my hands.

"You can't be sorry for him, Dabney."

"I'm not—it's just that—all this death and suicide and rot! I can't bear it. I can't bear anymore."

"He killed himself because he had syphilis, Dabney. The coroner told me so. It was destroying his mind and his nervous system and he knew what he'd end up like. But there's a funny addendum to all this."

"Funny? How can anything associated with Eugene Duckworth be funny?"

"It was his will that was funny—all his money, the Fairchild money he stole from Charlotte. Everyone in Virginia knows he forged her will. He left all that money to Belle Haven College to found the Duckworth Memorial Endowment Fund. Can you imagine, Dabney—that young ladies for ages to come will venerate Eugene Duckworth!"

I thought of Eugene and his dreary Lost Plantation Story, the vanished family grandeur and so on. The past had indeed driven him, but not in place of lust and greed, as he seemed to think. One could look at the way he lived and died and know that lust and greed would have driven him, even without the past. And what would his worthy, venerated ancestors have thought of syphilis? Still, I suppose in one sense Eugene could have considered himself a success: the Duckworths were restored to their rightful place as patrician benefactors. But the thought of young ladies of the ilk of Marjorie Vail paying their respects to someone as vile as Eugene Duckworth, venerating his memory, was just preposterous and I had to laugh. Laughter spilled out of me, bubbled forth, and so foreign was the sound of unrestrained laughter at Flintridge that the undermatron came running and burst into the office, and I laughed all the harder to see the look of shock upon her face. I wiped my eyes and told her it was nothing, and she left us, muttering. Bay and I recovered ourselves slowly, facing each other in the children's chairs.

"I've got some less humorous news, too," he said at last. "My mother died a month ago."

"I'm sorry, Bay."

"She was peaceful at the end and death was a release. It comes to all of us, Dabney. It's the price we pay."

"You sound like Austin. The wages of sin."

"No. The wages of life. Life, Dabney—it's all we have and we have to use it as best we can. You're wasting yours here, in this—" he glanced at the Bibles lining the shelves, the narrow ruler laid out on Miss Baum's desk, the grim walls and curtainless windows—"this place. You're letting your life go by without the one thing that can give it meaning."

"Bay—please don't."

"You can't make me leave this time. You're coming with me."

"Oh Bay—I can't. I can't—"

"I've thought it all out for nearly a year now. Don't you see—if we renounce our love in the name of the past, we're fools—fools! We can't let that happen. I won't hear any more talk of cinder and ashes and suicides, nothing more of Belle Haven and Charlotte Courtney—all that's finished. You're coming with me."

"I could never go back."

"I'm not going back. I've left Oakstone. I'm joining a practice in Washington, D.C., with a friend from medical school. You and I need never go back and we never will." He came towards me and peeled the mittens from my hands as he had peeled the bandages the winter before. He pressed my hands to his warm, familiar beard, and his hazel eyes roamed over me with a hunger and intensity I'd forgotten was possible. "You love me. You know you love me."

"I've always loved you."

He kissed my scarred hands and drew me to my feet and pressed me to his body. I recognized the moment for what it was, recognized it because in all these many months I'd unknowingly rehearsed it behind the curtains of my mind. All the time I thought I was only reliving the past, I was, in truth, rehearsing the future, because the future and the past are one—like the waters of a lake, they meld indistinguishably into each other, and our lives in the present are but fragile leaf boats, swirling, at any given moment, towards one shore or the other.

19

Now, of course, all these years later, I am rowing towards the final shore. Bay died last year. I didn't cry. My five sons stood by the grave weeping. One or the other of them stayed with me for weeks and weeks, waiting for me to purge myself of grief with tears and still I didn't cry. Finally I said to them: why should I cry? I've had more love, more life, more happiness with your father than I ever dreamed possible. Your father and I knew his end was coming. My end is coming too and I don't want you to grieve for me. I got all of you into this world and grown up and watched your families grow, and I've taken pride and pleasure in all of you. Yes, and I've given that pride and pleasure too. We are a family: connected by blood and the bonds of time and love, and these are the bonds that will surpass the grave. So, don't weep for me, I tell them.

But I never told them about Belle Haven. Our sons believe we met when Bay was attending me after an unfortunate fire I'd been in and they seemed satisfied with that. Our lie—or more correctly, our equivocation—was probably unnecessary; the past couldn't have mattered to them. Indeed, as the years passed, it mattered less and less to us. But I am still compelled to try to make sense of it as best I can. To understand the past is something one must do for oneself; it's a duty, one of the responsibilities—along with loving—of being human. Without love and an understanding of the past we're no better than the beasts in the field. But with love and understanding we are ennobled somehow, not quite angels perhaps, but then, who among us would exchange mere wings for love and all its bountiful pleasures?